"Are you wi
chance that
responsible for this to g
to stop before he reaches the
end of the legend?"

"No." The word fell from her lips in a grudging whisper.

"Look, I know you don't particularly want to be here, but you need to be someplace safe until we figure out who is behind all this. The bad news is, I'm not a great host. The good news is, I'm not home much."

Clay's words should have assured her, but they didn't. "I just feel like I'm imposing." In truth, even though she had only spent a single night and half a day here, she already felt ill at ease.

But it wasn't because he might be a poor host, it was because having seen the bed where he slept, she wanted to sleep there, too. It was because her desire for Clay James was reaching a proportion that was getting more and more difficult to ignore.

Dear Reader,

The year may be coming to a close, but the excitement never flags here at Silhouette Intimate Moments. We've got four—yes, four—fabulous miniseries for you this month, starting with Carla Cassidy's CHEROKEE CORNERS and *Trace Evidence,* featuring a hero who's a crime scene investigator and now has to investigate the secrets of his own heart. Kathleen Creighton continues STARRS OF THE WEST with *The Top Gun's Return.* Tristan Bauer had been declared dead, but now he was back—and very much alive, as he walked back into true love Jessie Bauer's life. Maggie Price begins LINE OF DUTY with *Sure Bet* and a sham marriage between two undercover officers that suddenly starts feeling extremely real. And don't miss *Nowhere To Hide,* the first in RaeAnne Thayne's trilogy THE SEARCHERS. An on-the-run single mom finds love with the FBI agent next door, but there are still secrets to uncover at book's end.

We've also got two terrific stand-alone titles, starting with Laurey Bright's *Dangerous Waters.* Treasure hunting and a shared legacy provide the catalyst for the attraction of two opposites in an irresistible South Pacific setting. Finally, Jill Limber reveals *Secrets of an Old Flame* in a sexy, suspenseful reunion romance.

Enjoy—and look for more excitement next year, right here in Silhouette Intimate Moments.

Yours.

Leslie J. Wainger
Executive Editor

Please address questions and book requests to:
Silhouette Reader Service
U.S.: 3010 Walden Ave., P.O. Box 1325, Buffalo, NY 14269
Canadian: P.O. Box 609, Fort Erie, Ont. L2A 5X3

Trace Evidence
CARLA CASSIDY

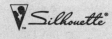

INTIMATE MOMENTS™

Published by Silhouette Books

America's Publisher of Contemporary Romance

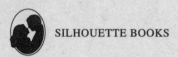 **SILHOUETTE BOOKS**

ISBN 0-373-27331-2

TRACE EVIDENCE

Copyright © 2003 by Carla Bracale

Visit Silhouette at www.eHarlequin.com

Printed in U.S.A.

Books by Carla Cassidy

CARLA CASSIDY

is an award-winning author who has written over fifty books for Silhouette. In 1995, she won Best Silhouette Romance from *Romantic Times* for *Anything for Danny*. In 1998, she also won a Career Achievement Award for Best Innovative Series from *Romantic Times*.

Carla believes the only thing better than curling up with a good book to read is sitting down at the computer with a good story to write. She's looking forward to writing many more books and bringing hours of pleasure to readers.

Chapter 1

"Got a job for you, Clay."

Clay James looked up from the microscope where he'd been studying a piece of fiber found on the latest murder victim of the killer who the local newspapers had dubbed the Shameless Slasher.

He frowned irritably at Glen Cleberg, the chief of police in the small Oklahoma city of Cherokee Corners. "I'm in the middle of something here. Whatever it is, can't you get somebody else to take care of it? I'm trying to identify a fiber found on Sam McClane's body."

He was certain that would make Glen leave the small police lab and him alone. The chief had been chewing on his butt to find something, anything that might clue them into the killer's identity before a third murder took place.

"As important as what you're doing is, I still need you on this other case."

Clay shut off the high-powered microscope, fighting against the foul mood that seemed to grip him tighter and stronger minute by minute, day by day. "What other case?"

"A break-in at the high school."

"Since when do we process something like that?" Clay interrupted impatiently. He had a hell of a lot more important things to deal with, like unsolved murders and a missing mother.

A stab of pain ripped through him as he thought of his mother, missing now for just over a month with few clues to follow to discover her whereabouts or if she were still alive or dead.

"Since the classroom that was broken into belongs to Tamara Greystone," Glen replied.

Tamara Greystone, local artist, teacher and Cherokee Corners' claim to fame. The fact that she was Native American, like Clay himself, and a close friend of the mayor's family was about all Clay knew about the woman.

"Clay, it's already after seven, past time for you to knock off for the day. If you'd just go by the school and check things out, you'll keep the mayor off my ass. He'll be happy to know I have my top man on the job."

Fighting a weary sigh, Clay nodded and stored away the specimen he'd been studying. Maybe some time away from the lab would give him a new perspective.

For the past two weeks he'd been putting in fourteen-hour days, studying, analyzing and cataloging trace evidence from the two murder scenes. That didn't count the time he was putting in on his mother's case. A little break away from the lab and intense work might be good for him.

"I'm on my way," he told his boss, who grunted and disappeared from the lab door.

Within fifteen minutes Clay was in his van and headed toward the high school on the outskirts of town. The July sun was still hot and he could almost taste the dust in the air, stirred up by a faint evening breeze.

He flipped the air conditioner in the van on high and tried to empty his head of thought. But that process had been next to impossible since the night almost six weeks ago when somebody had come into his parents' house and nearly killed his father, Thomas, with a blow to the back of his head.

Clay's mother, Rita Birdsong James, had been nowhere to be found. A suitcase had been missing along with some of her clothes and personal toiletries. The official speculation had been that Thomas and Rita had had one of their legendary fights and this time things had spiraled way out of control. The authorities believed Rita had hit her husband, then panicked and ran.

The James siblings had known that was impossible. As much as their mother, a beautiful, petite Cherokee woman, and their father, a big, brawny Irishman had fussed and yelled, screamed and cursed each other, it was merely part of their chemistry.

Rita and Thomas James had loved each other as passionately as they'd fought with one another. There was no way one could harm the other.

If that wasn't enough to fill his mind, there were the two murders to stew about. Greg Maxwell and Sam McClane had both been stabbed to death and left naked. Greg's body had been found in front of the public library and Sam had been left behind the post office.

They had been vicious killings, filled with rage and there had been little left on and around the bodies to aid Clay and the other crime-scene investigators in finding clues to the killer.

He felt as if in both cases he was fighting the ticking hand of a time bomb. If they didn't find his mother in time, she would probably eventually be found dead. And if he didn't find who the serial killer was, there was going to be more bodies.

Ticking time bombs, that's what he had on his hands and nothing was falling into place as it should. He tightened his hands on the steering wheel in frustration.

As the high school came into view, all thoughts of his mother and the serial killer fled from his mind. Two patrol cars were already in the parking lot and Clay shook his head as he pulled up and parked next to one of them.

Apparently it paid to be friends with the mayor. He could never remember a break-in anywhere that had warranted two cop cars and a crime-scene investigator…not in this small town.

Tamara Greystone must have pulled a handful of strings to get this kind of response. She was a big fish in a little pond here and he had a feeling she was probably one of those self-important divas in the art world.

He got out of his van and grabbed the metal suitcase that sometimes felt like an extension of his body. His irritation level had just ratcheted up to a dangerous degree.

The Cherokee Corners High School was a two-story brick building, with wide front steps that led up to the front door.

Clay had gone to high school here seventeen years ago. His high school days hadn't been awful, but they hadn't been terrific, either.

At the top of the stairs, Burt Creighton stood next to the door, looking bored and out of place in his khaki police uniform. He greeted Clay with a wry grin. "I joined the police department looking for danger and excitement. What do I get? An assignment to stand on the high school steps in the dying heat of the day."

"Why are you stationed here? Summer school has been over for several hours."

Burt shrugged. "Apparently Ms. Greystone teaches an adult education class at seven on Tuesday and Thursday nights. The class members have been arriving and I've been getting each person's name and address before sending them back home."

Clay shifted his kit from one hand to the other. "Seems like a lot of trouble for a classroom break-in. Who's inside?"

"Ed Rogers. He's guarding the classroom door, making sure nobody goes in until after you're finished in there."

"Anyone else there?"

"Ms. Greystone and that's it. It's room 230."

Clay nodded and entered the building. He was instantly assailed by scents of the distant past...the smell of chalk and teenage sweat, of industrial floor polish and bathroom deodorizer.

He took the stairs to the second floor two at a time, a new irritation growing inside with each step he took.

This was ridiculous, to be called here to process what was probably a simple case of classroom vandalism by some disgruntled student.

He had so many more important things to be doing...like trying to find his mother...like trying to find a serial killer. He didn't give a damn who Tamara Greystone thought she was, this was a waste of his time.

Ed Rogers greeted him at the top of the stairs. He motioned down the hallway. "Room 230 is on the left. Ms. Greystone is in room 231 across the hall. I wrote up a report, but I doubt we'll ever find out who did this unless some tough guy decides to brag."

Clay nodded. He'd already come to that conclusion. Still, he had a job to do. He headed down the hall, his heels silent against the polished tile floor.

Although he would have preferred to go directly to work, he turned into classroom 231 first. She stood, facing the doorway as if she'd heard his silent approach.

His first impression of her was one of grace and delicate beauty. She wore a traditional calico Cherokee tear dress. The dress had three quarter length sleeves and fell to her calves. It was sky blue with red-diamond-shaped accents around the yoke.

Her long hair was coiled in a careless knot at the nape of her neck, but it was her eyes that captured his attention more than anything. Large and more gray than black, they radiated kindness and peace. She certainly didn't look like an arrogant, artist diva.

"You must be Officer James." She took a step toward him and help out her hand. "I'm Tamara Greystone."

"Nice to meet you," he said as he gave her slender

hand a quick shake, then released it. "I understand there's been a break-in into your classroom. What can you tell me about it?"

Clay liked to get as much information as he could before he actually processed a scene. He never knew what tidbit of information a victim might tell him that would reveal a clue to what he saw and discerned from the crime scene itself. He gestured her to a nearby student chair.

Once she was seated, he took the chair next to hers and withdrew a pad and pen from his pocket. Even with the distance between them, he could smell her. The scent was earthy and mysterious. It surprised him. He couldn't remember the last time he'd noticed the scent of a woman.

"There really isn't much I can tell you," she said. "I left the school this afternoon just after four and went home. The classroom was fine at that time. I returned this evening just after six and found the room had been destroyed."

"Was anyone here when you left at four?" He kept his gaze focused on his pad.

"I think I was the last one out. I usually am. We have three periods of classes for summer school. Math is at ten, English is at noon and my class is at two." She offered him a smile that curved the corners of her full lips.

"What about the cleaning crew?" He looked back down at his pad, finding her smile far too appealing. What was wrong with him? First her smell, then her smile. For some reason he was finding her very distracting.

"The cleaning crew consists of Vernon Colby. He doesn't come in until about nine and works through the night. I'm not sure what his schedule is during the summer months.''

"Vernon Colby? I didn't know he was still alive.'' He'd been cleaning the high school when Clay had gone to classes here, and Clay had thought him ancient then.

"Have you had a fight with any of the students? Flunked anyone who might have a temper?'' he continued with the questions.

"No. Nothing like that.'' She shook her head, making tendrils of her dark hair come loose. "Well, technically most of the summer school students are in the class because they've flunked a class or need an additional credit to graduate.''

He wondered if those tendrils would feel like silk between his fingers. Clay put his pad and pen away, recognizing that whatever other information he needed would probably be in the official report Ed had written up.

Besides, he needed to get out of here and away from her.

"I'll just get to work now.'' He picked up his kit and headed out of the room and across the hall.

Maybe he was having some sort of a mini-breakdown, he thought. He'd never found a woman who could hold his attention like an intriguing crime scene.

He'd expected overturned desks, torn books, perhaps a smashed window or two, but when he looked into room 230, shock held him momentarily motionless.

He'd seen vandalism before, but nothing to the extent of what lay before him. Desks were not only overturned, but also smashed and broken into pieces.

Torn books and papers littered the floor like confetti after a parade.

The blackboard was cracked in half, but it was none of these things that sent a shock of adrenaline racing through him. What captured and held his attention were the marks that slashed high across the walls. Deep, gouging marks that were red with what appeared to be fresh blood.

Any irritation he'd felt about being sent here vanished as he stepped into the classroom and pulled a camera from his kit, the woman across the hall already forgotten.

This was where he came alive—in the middle of the chaos of a crime scene. Work was his life, and when he worked was the only time the anger inside him subsided, the only time the guilt silenced, the only time he was at peace within himself.

She watched him from the doorway as he walked around the room, taking pictures of the damage from every point of view. Tamara Greystone knew far more about Clay James than he thought he knew about her.

She'd worked with his mother at the Cherokee Cultural Center and Rita had often confided in Tamara her worry about her eldest child.

He was a sinfully handsome man, with rich black hair and sculptured features that were traditionally Native American—high cheekbones and a proud, strong nose, dark straight brows over intense black eyes. He had thin lips that appeared to have never curved upward in a smile.

Tall and lean, he had shoulders just broad enough to hint at wiry strength. As he moved around the room he displayed a natural, sleek grace that belied the fact that she knew he spent most of his days cooped up in a laboratory.

"Quite a mess, isn't it?" she said.

He started, as if he'd forgotten her presence, and it was obvious from his look of irritation that he'd like to continue to forget her presence. "Yeah, it's a mess."

He put the camera down on the metal suitcase he'd carried in and looked at her once again. "There's really nothing more you can do here. You're free to go on home."

"Thank you, but I'll stay until you're finished."

His frown turned from irritated to positively daunting. "Look, Ms. Greystone. It really would be best if you'd just leave me to do my job."

"That's exactly what I intend to do." She smiled. "Surely you understand my need to be here. I'm sure if somebody had come into your lab and done something like this, no matter who was processing the scene, you'd want to be there. This is more than just the place where I work, Officer James. This classroom is a part of my heart."

"Then just stay out of my way," he said curtly.

"I'll do that." She remained standing in the doorway as he got back to work.

The initial horror of what had been done to the room had worn off, but the senseless, extensive damage still sent a small wave of disquiet through her.

Who could have done this? And why? She'd always tried so hard to maintain good relationships with her fellow teachers and students.

She focused her gaze at Clay, watching as he studied the marks on the walls. He seemed completely and totally absorbed in his work. That's part of what had bothered Rita about her son. According to Rita, her only son had no life beyond work, had turned his back on his Native heritage and had become a bitter, angry man with a chip on his shoulder.

The chip wasn't visible at the moment, but his total concentration on his work was apparent. She knew he'd forgotten about her as he scraped bits of the material that looked like blood into a vial.

She supposed his total absorption in his work was what made him so good at what he did. Rita had always overworried about all her children, not only Clay, but also his sisters, Breanna and Savannah.

Rita. Thoughts of the missing woman filled her with grief. She missed seeing Rita's beautiful face at the Cherokee Cultural Center, missed her exuberance and enthusiasm for the work and education that the cultural center afforded their community.

"These look like some sort of animal claws," he said as he studied the marks that rode high on the walls.

"How would an animal have gotten in here?" she asked.

"No animal has been in this room," he said in direct counter to his previous statement. "If an animal had been loose in here there'd be additional signs, such as odors and waste material."

"Then how did the claw marks get there?"

He frowned. "That's what I need to figure out."

"If animal claws made the marks, can you tell what kind of animal it might be?"

"Not just by looking at them. I'll have to take plaster casts and get them back to the lab to do some comparison study. There are bits of fur embedded in the marks, so that will make identification easier."

Apparently he'd talked himself out, because for the next hour he didn't say another word. That was fine with Tamara. Silence never bothered her. Her parents had taught her as a child that silence was to be respected and revered. It was a time to observe and learn from what was inside you and what surrounded you.

Clay James was far more interesting to watch than listening to her inner thoughts. He radiated a fierce intensity, a focus that was assuring. She had no doubt that his expertise and tenacity would eventually identify the culprit.

"That's all I can do here," he finally said as he packed up his samples and tools. "Have you spoken to Will Nichols and let him know what's going on?"

Will Nichols was the principal of the high school. "Yes, I called him. He stopped by earlier, saw the damage and told me to keep him posted."

"You won't be teaching in this room any time soon. I want it left locked for the next couple of days in case I need to come back and take some more samples."

"I noticed you didn't try to get any fingerprints."

His jaw muscle tightened, as if he thought she was questioning his expertise. "It's pointless to print a room where so many people pass through on a regular basis. If this had been a murder scene, or the scene of an assault, then I might have considered it. But this room could potentially hold the prints of students that had passed through over the years. It would take us months to find out who they belong to." His gaze was cold as it met hers. "Is there anything else you think I've forgotten?"

Prickly, she thought. Definitely prickly. "Officer

James, I wouldn't begin to tell you how to do your job. Just as I wouldn't expect you to come into my classroom and take over my job.'' She offered him a smile. ''I just watch a lot of television and it seems on the crime shows everyone is always taking fingerprints.''

He grabbed his kit and walked toward where she stood in the doorway. ''You shouldn't believe everything you see on TV.''

He turned off the light in the room and watched as she locked the door. ''I have a spare key.'' She fumbled with her key chain until she worked a key off the ring. She held it out to him. ''This way if you need to get back inside, day or night, you have access as long as somebody can unlock the front school door for you.''

He took the key from her and slid it into the back pocket of his tight jeans. Together they walked down the silent hallway toward the stairs. Ed and Burt had both stuck their heads in the classroom earlier to tell Clay they'd questioned Vernon and they were leaving.

Vernon Colby was waiting for them by the front door. ''Damn fool kids...nothing but meanness in them nowadays,'' he muttered as he unlocked the door for Clay and Tamara to exit.

Night had fallen outside and overhead the bright, sparkly stars were companions to a three-quarter moon. Parked in the lot were two vehicles, the van that Clay had driven and the rusted-out pickup that belonged to Vernon.

''Where's your car?'' he asked.

''I don't drive to school,'' she replied. ''I always

walk to and from work. It's just a little over a mile walk.''

He raked a hand through his thick hair and stared out into the darkness of the night. ''I'll drive you home.'' It was obvious it wasn't something he particularly looked forward to doing.

''That isn't necessary,'' she demurred. ''I'm used to walking home and the darkness doesn't frighten me.''

''It should,'' he snapped. ''You should be afraid of what the darkness holds. People can be perfectly safe in their own homes one minute, then dead or missing in the next.''

She knew that he was talking about what happened to his parents and her heart went out to him. But she had a feeling that Clay James was a man who didn't appreciate empty platitudes.

''Thank you, I'll accept the offer of a ride home,'' she said.

He opened the passenger door for her and she slid inside. The interior of the van smelled like him, a combination of clean-scented cologne and breath mints.

He got in and started the van. ''Which way?''

She pointed to the left. ''Go down the road about a half a mile. There's a dirt road. Turn right there and I'm at the end of the road.''

He didn't speak again until they turned on the dirt road where thick trees crowded in from either side. ''I didn't even know this was here,'' he said.

''Most people don't. I found it two years ago when I returned to Cherokee Corners from New York. I like the woods and the solitude.''

He slowed as they came to the end of the road, and

his headlights shone on the little cabin she called home. A faint light shone from behind the living room curtains.

"I know it doesn't look like much," she said. "But it's a perfect artist retreat, an adequate home and holds a sense of spiritual peace that is comforting."

"You don't have to apologize to me for your living conditions," he said as he pulled to a halt before the place.

"On the contrary, Officer James, I wasn't apologizing. I was merely trying to make pleasant conversation."

She hesitated a moment, then continued. "I'm sure you've put in a long day. Would you like to come in for a cup of coffee?" She wasn't sure what had prompted the invitation. He certainly hadn't been overly sociable and there was no reason for any further contact with him.

He stared at the cabin for a long moment, then, to her surprise shut off his van engine and turned to look at her. "A cup of coffee sounds good."

Chapter 2

He had no idea why he'd agreed to go inside her home and drink a cup of coffee. Maybe because he didn't want to go back to the lab just yet. Maybe because he didn't want to go to his own home, which would be far too silent and allow him far too many thoughts and recriminations.

"It's pretty isolated out here," he observed as they walked up the three steps that led to a long front porch. The small cabin was in the center of a copse of thick trees and brush.

She laughed, the sound echoing like birdsong in the air.

"That's the difference between a cop and an artist. A cop sees isolated, an artist sees secluded."

Despite the irritation that had filled him earlier, he felt himself relax a bit, as if the pleasant sound of her laughter had worked like a balm on a sore wound.

"A cop sees lots of hiding places. I suppose you see lots of things to paint, Ms. Greystone."

"Exactly, and please call me Tamara." She unlocked her door and pushed it open. "Welcome to my secluded little cabin in the woods."

He stepped into the door and felt as if he'd been swept into a different world, a different universe. The room was a visual wonderland filled with shapes and colors.

The beige sofa held an array of throw pillows in a variety of colors. Paintings covered the walls and a half-finished one rested on an easel in front of a side window that would catch the morning light.

Roughhewn shelves held pottery and woven baskets in all shapes and sizes and a collection of hummingbirds set on top of the fireplace mantle. Fresh wildflowers were in vases everywhere and the room was scented with their sweet fragrance.

The total effect should have been chaotic and cluttered, but instead the room radiated a sense of balance and serenity

As he looked around, taking it all in, he felt some of the day's pressures easing. His shoulder muscles seemed to unkink a little and the burn that had smoldered in the pit of his stomach for the last month dissipated somewhat.

"Please, come on into the kitchen and I'll put the coffee on."

He followed her into a cozy kitchen as colorful and unique as the living room. She gestured him to a small wooden table, then busied herself with the coffeemaker.

He noticed a shelf above the kitchen sink filled

with healthy plants of various types. "You must have quite a green thumb," he said.

"I like growing things."

He leaned back in the surprisingly comfortable wooden chair and viewed her from top to bottom, taking in the length of her slender back and the curve of shapely hips beneath the dress. "I'm surprised we haven't run into each other before now."

She turned from the coffeepot and flashed him a grin. "I try not to run into the police, Officer James."

"Call me Clay," he said. "Whenever you say Mr. or Officer James, I think you're talking to my father."

"All right, then Clay it is. And I don't go into town very often, just when I need groceries or art supplies and occasionally to visit with Alyssa at the Redbud."

He looked at her in surprise. "You know my cousin Alyssa?"

"She and I have become good friends recently, since I moved back from New York. I try to have her to dinner out here at least once every couple of weeks."

"That's nice. Alyssa could use more friends. So, you didn't like the Big Apple?"

She hesitated a moment before replying. "No…it wasn't my cup of tea." There was something in her tone that forbid him to ask any more questions on that particular topic.

"But you're originally from Cherokee Corners?" He was aware that he was talking more to her than he'd talked to anyone in the last several weeks, but she was easy to talk to. Something about her soft, seemingly accepting demeanor invited conversation.

"Born and raised here. You were several years older than me, so we didn't run in the same crowd."

"What's with the hummingbirds?" he asked, noting that several glass figurines hung at the window over the sink.

"The hummingbird is one of my totem animals."

He was grateful when she didn't elaborate. He didn't want to hear about totems and spirituality, about old Cherokee ways and the voice of the elders. It was these kinds of things that he'd fought about with his mother just before she'd disappeared.

He was suddenly sorry he'd followed his impulse to come inside, but now that the coffee was finished brewing, he wasn't sure how to leave gracefully. Just one fast cup, then I'm out of here, he thought.

As she reached up high in a cabinet to pull down two stoneware mugs, he couldn't help but notice the slender curve of her calves beneath the length of her dress.

Although he'd tried his best to immerse himself in his work as he'd taken samples and photographed her classroom, he'd been acutely conscious of her presence the entire time. Not only had her exotic fragrance gone directly to his head, but he'd been impressed by her quiet and calm in the face of such devastation.

"I appreciate you not being one of those hysterical women," he said as she sat a mug of steaming coffee before him.

"Cream or sugar?" He shook his head negatively and she joined him at the table. "What's to be hysterical about? What's done is done. My screaming and yelling wouldn't have put the classroom back in order. I'm just sorry so many of the books appeared to have been torn up. It will be months before we can get more books and then only if extra money can be squeezed out of the budget.''

He took a sip of the coffee. It was good—hot and strong the way he liked it. ''You said you watched a lot of television, but I noticed there wasn't a TV in the living room.''

She smiled and the beauty of that smile hit him square in the pit of his stomach. ''Ah, you've discovered my guilty pleasure. I have a little ten-inch set in my bedroom and am notorious for watching it for a couple of hours before I fall asleep.'' Her dark eyes gazed at him for a long moment. ''But I'm sure you've been far too busy lately to even think about television programming.''

''Yeah, it's been a long six weeks.''

''Any breaks in your mother's disappearance?''

''Not really, although my sister Savannah found two cases in Oklahoma that are so similar it's eerie.''

''Really?'' She leaned forward and he caught another whiff of her scent.

''In fact, one of those cases is what brought Savannah and her fiancé, Riley, together.'' He took another sip of his coffee, wishing she'd lean back in her chair so he couldn't smell her, so he couldn't see the dark length of her eyelashes, the dewy moisture of her lips.

What on earth was wrong with him? Why was Tamara Greystone making him think of things he hadn't thought of in a very long time…like hot, eager kisses and silky hair tangled around his fingers, and warm, slender curves pressed against his body? Why was he talking so much when normally he had nothing much to say to anyone?

For just a moment, as he'd looked into her large,

dark gray eyes, the pain, the anger, the uncertainty that had ruled his life for so long had momentarily ebbed. He reached for it now, the pain chasing away any inexplicable desire he might feel for Tamara.

"Two years ago Riley Frazier's mother disappeared under the same kind of circumstances as my mother. Riley's father had been hit over the head. Unfortunately, he was killed. Riley's mother was nowhere to be found. Some of her clothing was missing and the police assumed she was responsible for Riley's father's death."

"Sounds exactly like what happened to your parents, although thankfully your father wasn't killed."

Clay nodded, and swallowed hard against the knot of emotion that twisted in him at thoughts of his mother. He remembered that night almost six weeks ago when he'd been called to his parents' ranch. His father had been taken away in an ambulance and his mother hadn't been anywhere to be found. He'd known then that something terrible had happened not only to his father, but to his mother as well.

"True, although he's still recuperating. Unfortunately, he doesn't remember anything about that night. Anyway, Riley's mother's body was found a week ago in Sycamore Ridge on some property he was excavating for building a home."

"How tragic," Tamara replied. "Did anyone find out what had happened to her?"

"According to the medical examiner, she'd been dead for about four months."

"Four months…but didn't you say she went missing two years ago?"

Clay nodded. "We don't know what happened to

her between the time of her disappearance and the time of her murder.''

''Murder?'' Tamara's voice was a soft whisper.

''Yeah, her skull was smashed in, just like her husband's had been two years before.''

Tamara wrapped her fingers around her mug. He noticed that her fingers were long and slender, and her nails just long enough to be completely feminine. ''You said three cases. What's the third?''

''Two years before Riley Frazier's mother went missing a woman in Sequoia Falls also disappeared under the same exact circumstances. The husband was hit over the head and killed, and she was gone, along with some of her personal belongings. She still hasn't been found.''

''So, maybe she's still alive. Just like it's possible your mother is still alive.'' Her voice rang with hope that he desperately wanted to grab on to.

''That's the only thought that keeps me getting up in the morning.'' He took another drink of the coffee, then continued, ''I feel like I'm working against a bomb with a ticking clock, but the problem is I don't know who set the timer, or how much time is left. I just feel so damned helpless.'' Again, he felt a ball of emotion pressing tight against his chest.

She reached across the table and lightly touched one of his hands. ''You'll find her, Clay.''

He pulled his hand from her touch, finding it not only distracting, but disturbing as well. The touch had been too warm, too soft.

He took a drink of his coffee, his thoughts returning to his mother. Yes, eventually he'd find her, but would he find her in time? Would he find her dead or alive?

And what in the hell was he doing here sipping coffee and baring his soul to a woman he didn't know at all?

Tamara could tell the exact moment he turned off. His black eyes went blank and his jaw muscles tightened and she knew their conversation had come to a halt. Sure enough, he downed the last drop of coffee from his mug and stood.

"Thanks for the coffee," he said. "I've got to get going."

She followed him to the front door. Even his walk looked uptight despite the fact that she couldn't help but notice that his jeans fit quite nicely on his long legs and rear end.

"One of the other officers will be in touch with you when they have anything on the vandalism."

"Thank you, Clay, for all your help."

"Just doing my job," he replied as he stepped out of the door. "Good night, Tamara."

"Good night, Clay."

She stood on her front porch long after his van had disappeared from sight.

It had been a long time since she'd felt a spark of physical attraction toward a man. But the moment Clay had stepped into the classroom and introduced himself, she'd felt a definite spark of warmth deep in the pit of her stomach.

The last time she'd found herself physically attracted to a man she'd allowed herself to be swept into a relationship that had not only ended in heartache, but had also left her questioning her values and the very essence of who she was.

She looked up at the moon peeping through the

branches of the ancient trees. Good old Maxwell
Bishop. He'd been her agent for six months before
they had become lovers. He'd done amazing things
for her career as an artist, but in the four months they
had been a couple, he'd nearly destroyed her self-
identity.

According to everything she'd heard about Clay,
he'd be a danger to her in much the same way. This
was one particular spark she intended to ignore.

Not that it mattered. Clay had made it quite clear
that others would handle her case from here on out.
Cherokee Corners wasn't that small a town. The odds
of her and Clay running into each other again were
minimal.

Reluctantly, she left the night air and went back
inside the cabin. She had just finished washing the
coffee mugs to put back in the cabinet when the
phone rang.

She hurried from the kitchen to the sofa and picked
up the cordless from the end table. "Hello?"

"Are you all right?" Alyssa Whitefeather's voice
filled the line.

"Bad news travels fast in this town," Tamara replied. "How did you hear about it?"

"I heard between a hot fudge sundae and a banana
split." Alyssa owned the Redbud Bed and Breakfast.
The top two floors of her establishment were guest
rooms and the bottom floor was Alyssa's living quar-
ters and an ice cream parlor. "Burt Creighton stopped
in for a cup of coffee and was talking about the mess
in your classroom."

"It was a mess," Tamara agreed.

"You must have been terrified when you saw it."

Tamara thought of that moment when she'd first

viewed the vandalized room. "Actually, it didn't scare me at all," she said. "Mostly I just felt sad for whomever had done such a terrible thing."

"Well, it frightened me when I heard about it," Alyssa replied.

There was something in her friend's voice that sent a flutter of disquiet through Tamara. "Why? Have you seen something, Alyssa?"

Alyssa laughed, the laughter sounding forced. "Oh, you know me. I'm the local nutcase in town. I'm always seeing things that aren't there, having visions that don't make sense. I should probably be on medication."

"Having a pity party, are we?"

This time Alyssa's laugh was genuine. "Maybe a little one," she admitted. "It's just been a bad week," she added.

Tamara heard the weariness in her friend's voice. Over the course of their friendship Alyssa had confided in Tamara that she'd always suffered visions. Since Rita James's disappearance the visions had increased in frequency and intensity.

"I'll tell you what I think you need," Tamara said. "You need dinner tomorrow night with a friend."

"I can't do that," Alyssa protested. "Friday nights are the busiest of the week in the ice cream parlor."

Tamara frowned thoughtfully. She knew there was no way she could talk Alyssa into closing up shop on a Friday night. "Okay, then how about we meet at the café about four. You can get back to work by five or five-thirty when your Friday night rush usually begins."

"That sounds good," Alyssa replied after a moment of hesitation. "I could use a little break. So, I'll see you tomorrow about four. And Tamara, do me a favor and be extra careful.''

"Don't you worry about me. I'm fine."

With a murmur of goodbyes, the two hung up. It was getting late enough Tamara knew she should go to bed, but her head was too filled with thoughts to allow sleep.

She got up from the sofa and went into the small bedroom. She took off the traditional tear dress and hung it in the closet next to half a dozen others. She usually only wore the dresses on Tuesday and Thursday evenings when she taught her adult Native American cultural classes, or for special occasions and ceremonies.

She pulled on her nightie, a short yellow silk sheath with spaghetti straps, then returned to the kitchen for a glass of ice water.

While she sat at the table, a nice light breeze breathed through the window to caress her. The cabin had no air-conditioning except a window unit in the bedroom. She rarely ran it, preferring her windows opened and the sweet, forest-scented night air coming inside.

But tonight, with Alyssa's pressure for her to take care, she finished her ice water, then closed the window and locked it. She did the same with the other windows in the cabin, then went into her bedroom and turned the window unit air conditioner on low.

She got into bed, although thoughts still tumbled topsy-turvy through her head. She had no idea what to anticipate when she returned to school the next day. The only thing she knew for sure was that she would not be teaching classes in her own classroom.

She remembered Clay's question about students

she might have that might nurse a grudge against her. Nobody specific came to mind, but her class was filled with wise guys and underachievers.

There were also some gems in the class, students who were taking the summer classes in order to graduate early or to fill the long summer days.

It was the long summer nights that far too often lately filled Tamara with longing. She was thirty years old and more and more felt the desire for a family. But in order to have a family, she'd have to first find a good man and that had been a problem.

She'd become wary since her experience with Max. And in the two years since Max, she had mentally formed a picture of the kind of man she wanted in her life. Alyssa always told her no such man existed, that she was too picky and her expectations were too high.

She rolled over on her back and stared up at the ceiling, a vision of Clay James filling her mind. Physically, he was everything she'd ever hope to find in a man.

As she thought of the way his shoulders had filled out his shirt, the lean hips in those tight blue jeans, she could swear the temperature of the room rose by several degrees.

But she knew better than to get her hormones racing where Clay James was concerned. According to Alyssa the only thing that interested her cousin came in test tubes and evidence sample bags.

According to Clay's own mother he was an angry man who had turned his back on his Native American heritage. Tamara had attempted to do the same thing for four months to please the man she'd thought she'd loved, but she'd been unable to sustain the rejection of her Cherokee blood. She would never attempt it again.

No, Clay James wasn't her dream man, either. Her dream man was still out there somewhere, waiting for the winds of fate to bring them together. Tamara was a patient woman and she'd learned long ago not to try to hurry fate, but to accept each day as a gift.

Rita James had lost track of how many days she'd been held captive. She hadn't known how long she'd been unconscious, but when she'd finally come to and realized she was being held prisoner, she'd begun to keep track of the days by the meals that appeared through a slot in the steel door. Breakfast…sometimes lunch…and dinner…a day had passed.

But tonight she couldn't remember whether it had been twenty-two days or thirty-two days and the fact that she couldn't remember for sure frightened her as much as anything that had happened so far.

She feared she was losing her mind, and that was all she had left. Her beloved husband, Thomas, had been taken from her…murdered. She remembered seeing him lying motionless on their living room floor, blood everywhere. She knew he was dead, then she'd been grabbed from behind and that was the last thing she remembered until she'd awakened in this room.

This mockery of a room, she thought as she sat in the middle of the bed. When she'd first awakened from her drugged sleep, she'd thought she was at home in her own bed. The bedspread was the same, the bed was the same, even the nightstand and Tiffany-style lamp were the same as what she had in her own room.

However, this wasn't her room. Her bedroom had a window where sweet morning light crept in and moonlight whispered good-night. Her bedroom had no steel door with a lock. This was a stage setting…a facade, a fake built by a madman who held her hostage, a madman who had yet to tell her why she was here or what he wanted from her.

Initially she'd had hope. Her daughter Breanna was a vice cop, her other daughter, Savannah, a homicide detective and her son, Clay, was a crime-scene investigator. She'd hoped they would find her. She'd hoped there would be enough clues to lead them to her, but with each day that passed, her hope grew dimmer and dimmer.

Twenty-two days or thirty-two? How had she managed to lose track? Thomas…Thomas…her heart cried out for her husband and the life they'd shared together, the future they had anticipated spending together.

Even if she managed to get out of this windowless, locked room, even if eventually she was found, there would be no Thomas waiting for her.

Tears burned at her eyes as she realized no matter what happened, her life would never be the same again. Her tears were also for her children, who she knew must be suffering all kinds of agony trying to find out what had happened to her.

The sound of her sob was welcomed in this silent tomb. The utter silence of her days and nights had the potential to drive her utterly mad. She'd always been a woman who had valued a certain amount of silence, but this complete isolation was soul-damaging.

The only time she had any human contact at all was when the slot in the steel door would open and two black-gloved hands would slide in a tray of food.

Over and over again she'd begged him to say something to her, anything, her hunger for interaction so great. But no word was ever spoken. The tray slid in, the door slammed shut and she was once again left alone in the killing silence.

Help me to remain strong, she prayed. Eventually she would learn why she was being held here, what was wanted from her. The terror of the unknown was with her every minute of every day.

Please, please keep me strong. She knew sooner or later the madman with the black-gloved hands would show his face, would make demands and she prayed she would be strong enough to survive.

Chapter 3

Decorative rocks. Clay spent most of his morning chasing down names on lists of customers who had ordered the kind of decorative rocks he'd found around his father's chair in his parents' living room and in Riley Frazier's parents' living room.

It was the only real evidence he had from the two crime scenes that had left one man dead, one man severely wounded and two women missing. One of those women, Riley Frazier's mother, had since been found dead and Clay felt the pressure of trying to make sense of what little had been left behind at each crime scene.

He was still waiting for test results on trace evidence that had to be sent to a lab in Oklahoma City. But he knew the lab was backed up and it might be weeks before he got definitive test results.

"Clay?"

He looked up from the list of quarry customers he'd

obtained to see his sister Savannah standing in the doorway of the lab.

"You have any more for me on the McClane fiber?"

He nodded as his sister approached where he sat at his desk. "Unfortunately the only thing I can tell you is that it's one hundred percent cotton."

"That's it?" she asked, a frown creasing her brow.

"Afraid so." He sighed in frustration and raked a hand through his hair. "I've got a single fiber for you on a serial murder case and a handful of pebbles to try to find out what happened to Mom."

"You can only work with what you have, Clay," Savannah said softly. "That's all any of us can do."

"But it's not enough." Anger rose up inside him, the anger of utter impotence. Somehow, someway, he couldn't help but think somebody had missed something…a vital piece of evidence that might lead them to their mother.

"Glen should have let me process the scene initially," he said, his anger evident in his voice.

"You know that wasn't a good idea," Savannah said. "And you know your team is good. If there had been anything there to find, they would have found it."

"At least we have the rocks from Mom and Dad's house and from Riley's parents' home," he said. "Unfortunately, it's not much in the form of a smoking gun. We don't even know if the perpetrator of whatever has been going on with the missing women is from here, from Sycamore Ridge where the Frazier's lived, or from Sequoia Falls where the first incident occurred. Dammit, we don't have any idea at all what's going on."

Savannah laid a hand on his shoulder. "I know you're hurting, Clay. We're all hurting and we're all doing the best we can to find her."

Clay nodded, but he knew his pain was different from his sisters' pain. They hadn't fought with Rita the very last time they'd seen her alive.

They hadn't said things that needed to be left unsaid, that now might never get the chance to be unsaid. Savannah and Breanna missed her, were frightened for her, but they didn't live with the regrets that were slowly eating him alive.

"Have you had lunch?" she asked.

"Haven't had time."

"It's going to be dinnertime soon, why don't you give yourself a break and go get something to eat. Your brain doesn't function as well when your stomach is empty."

Clay stood from his desk, knowing she was right. His stomach had been growling for the past hour and the gnarl had become more and more difficult to ignore as time had passed.

He put away the reports he'd been reading from the quarries that had provided client lists, then left the small building that was an appendage to the back of the police station.

It had been six years ago, when Clay's father, Thomas, had been chief of police that Thomas had decided the small town needed its own crime-scene investigators and crime lab.

Thomas had been not only a great chief of police, but also a fine politician, who'd convinced the town of the need and had actively gone after private donations to get what he wanted.

One of the biggest donations had come from Jacob

Kincaid, owner of American Bank, the only bank in Cherokee Corners, and a good friend of Clay's parents.

In fact, Jacob was like an uncle to Clay and as he stepped onto the hot concrete of the sidewalk, he realized it had been too long since he and Jacob had talked.

Clay walked toward the café in the Center Square. It was a favorite eating establishment in town. Huge portions, reasonable prices and run by a woman named Ruby who claimed to be a descendent of the woman who'd run the first, most successful brothel in the state.

Lots of the cops ate there, but Clay definitely wasn't in the mood for company. The brief conversation with Savannah had stirred his guilt and the hundreds of regrets he'd lived with since the night of his mother's disappearance.

He just wanted to eat, then get back to the lab where work was piled up awaiting his attention. He already knew it was going to take hours to go over those lists from the quarries to find out who had ordered loads of that particular decorative rock.

The sun was hot on his shoulders, and the air smelled of city heat—smoked tires, hot oil and a faint overlay of spoiling garbage.

Clay hated summer, when tempers flared more quickly and crime rose drastically. He hated the dry hot wind that scorched the earth, then blew the ashes of dust everywhere.

He'd never felt a real connection to Cherokee Corners, except for that of his family. Even with them he felt a distance.

They were all into their own lives, with families

and loved ones and they all worked at the Cherokee Cultural Center in their spare time, a place Clay hadn't been to since he was thirteen.

It had been that fact that he and his mother had fought about the day before she'd disappeared. At the end of the summer, the cultural center always held a huge celebration where the entire town was invited. Rita had told him she wanted him to be a part of the ceremonies, that it was past time he took his place as a member of the Cherokee nation.

He had responded angrily with words that now he wished desperately he could take back.

By the time he reached the café his mood had turned darker than usual. It was just after four and he knew there wouldn't be much of a crowd in the café. It was too late for the lunch bunch and too early for the dinner crowd.

That was fine with him. All he wanted was a booth to himself, a good hot meal and a moment of peace to enjoy it.

"Ah, if it isn't my favorite CSI hunk," Ruby greeted him as he walked through the door. Ruby Majors was a big woman with a bleached blond bouffant that spoke of a different era.

"Hey, Ruby. What's good today?" he asked as he stopped by the register where she was seated.

"Randy's having a creative day. I'd stay away from the chicken surprise and the meat loaf medley. Anything else on the menu is great."

"Thanks for the heads-up. I'm just going to grab a booth in the back."

"Your cousin Alyssa is back there with that painter woman," Ruby said.

Tamara Greystone. He hesitated, unsure whether to

go forward or just take a seat at the counter where he knew he would eat in solitude.

The decision was taken out of his hand. Alyssa spied him and stood up and waved. He loved his cousin, who he believed was the only person in town who had a soul more tortured than his own.

Even though he wasn't in the mood to socialize, he drew a deep breath and ambled toward the booth where Alyssa and Tamara were having lunch.

"Clay." Alyssa rose and gave him a hug. "Please, join us." She sat back down and scooted over to give him room next to her.

"I was just going to grab something quick, then get back to work." He turned his attention to Tamara. "Hello, Tamara. Have you spoken with Officer Rogers today?" He slid into the booth next to Alyssa.

"No, should I have?"

She looked as pretty today as she had the night before. Today she was clad in a sleeveless yellow dress that set off the bronze tones of her skin and made her hair look like a black curtain of silk.

He'd had trouble sleeping last night because he couldn't get her out of his mind. He didn't like it and he didn't have time for it. "This morning I tested the blood from those claw marks that were in your classroom. Ed...I mean, Officer Rogers was supposed to get in touch with you and let you know it wasn't human blood. It was animal blood, probably deer."

"Well, that's a relief, I guess. I mean, I'm grateful it wasn't human, but I would have much preferred it to be ketchup."

"I haven't had a chance to check on the fur I found. Hopefully I can get to it in the next day or two," he said. He'd thought her eyes had looked pretty last night, but today they appeared even more gray, a startling but attractive foil to her dark hair and cinnamon skin. He started to stand. "And now I'll just let you two ladies finish your lunches."

Alyssa caught his arm and kept him from rising. "Don't run off. You might as well sit here and eat your meal with us instead of sitting all alone."

He could smell Tamara's perfume wafting in the air, the same subtle mysterious scent he'd found disturbing the night before. He didn't want to sit with them, but before he could think up any kind of an excuse, the waitress arrived to take his order.

"How's the case going?" Alyssa asked once the waitress had left the table.

"Which one? I'm working the serial case and, of course Mom's case and the usual other cases that come in. And now, the vandalism evidence from Tamara's classroom," he replied.

"I hope you aren't taking away time from the other two cases to worry about mine," Tamara said.

He didn't want to look at her because he liked looking at her. He couldn't remember ever being so aware of a woman as he was her. "I try to work every case as if it's top priority," he replied and gazed at a picture on the wall just over the top of her head.

"Anything new on your mom?" Alyssa asked.

He turned his focus on her. "Not really." He had told nobody but the chief of police that he'd discovered the same type of decorative pebbles around where his father had been hit and around where Riley Frazier's father had been killed. "I don't suppose you've had any helpful thoughts," he asked pointedly.

Alyssa smiled. "Tamara knows about my visions,

and unfortunately no, I haven't had any more about Aunt Rita other than the one I've told you about.''

''You mean the one where you see Mom in her own bedroom.''

Alyssa nodded and her smile no longer lifted the corners of her mouth. ''That's all I'm seeing of Aunt Rita, but I'm having a lot of other disturbing visions.''

''Want to talk about it?'' Tamara asked gently.

Alyssa shook her head. ''No.'' She forced a smile to her face. ''We're here to enjoy lunch, and it isn't every day that I get to have lunch with one of my cousins and one of my newest friends.''

Their meals arrived at the same time. Clay had ordered a burger and fries, Alyssa had ordered a tuna salad plate and Tamara had ordered a chef salad.

For most of the meal Clay remained silent, listening to the two women visit with each other. He'd grown up with two baby sisters, so having girl talk swirling around him was nothing new.

What was new was the fact that he found Tamara Greystone and everything that fell out of her mouth fascinating.

He knew as a teacher she would be smart, but he hadn't thought about her having a sense of humor. More than once she brought a smile to his face with something witty she said.

Brains, beauty and humor, she was a total package. A total package of trouble, he reminded himself. She was obviously a Native American woman in tune with the spiritual ties to her heritage.

He was a Native American man who wanted nothing to do with his heritage. Besides, he didn't have time for any relationship, had always found relationships difficult in the past.

He'd come to the realization a long time ago that he was a man who would in all probability spend his life alone. And he'd made peace with that probability.

He finished eating first. Explaining that he needed to get right back to work, he left the two of them seated at the table. He paid the tab for the three meals, then was almost out the door when he heard Alyssa calling his name.

He turned to see her hurrying toward him, her brow furrowed with worry. "Can I talk to you alone for just a minute?" she asked.

"Sure." He pulled her over by a coatrack where they would be out of the way of incoming and out-going diners. "What's up?"

"I didn't want to say anything in front of Tamara, but last night I had an awful vision concerning her."

Clay was ambivalent in his feelings concerning Alyssa's visions. On the one hand, he knew of more than one instance when her visions had helped solve a crime by finding a missing person and saving a life or two. On the other hand, he also knew she some-times had visions that never came true, never con-nected to anything and eventually went away.

"What was it about?" he asked.

"Tamara." Alyssa's eyes were troubled. "I saw her being chased by a monster and when the monster finally caught her, he…he ripped her heart out."

Clay put a hand on Alyssa's shoulder. "Alyssa, did you hear about the vandalism in Tamara's classroom before you had the vision?"

She nodded. "Ed Rogers came into the Redbud and had a cup of coffee last night. He told me all about it."

"Including the claw marks and the blood?" Again

she nodded and he squeezed her shoulder gently. "Then, isn't it possible hearing about that provoked that particular vision?"

"I suppose," Alyssa admitted after a moment of hesitation. "I just wanted to tell you. I was worried."

"Try not to worry, Alyssa. The vandalism in Tamara's classroom might not have even been directed at her specifically. Hers was one of the few unlocked classrooms in the school. It was probably simply a matter of convenience for the perps that her classroom got hit."

"You think?"

He offered her a tight smile. "Go back and finish enjoying your lunch. No monster is going to get to Tamara. I've got to get back to work."

"Thanks, Clay," Alyssa said.

He watched as she hurried back to the booth, then turned on his heel and headed out of the café, intent on putting Tamara Greystone out of his head.

"Your cousin is quite a handsome man," Tamara said when Alyssa returned to the table.

"Yeah, he is."

"How old is he?"

"Thirty-five," Alyssa said. She gazed at Tamara with narrowed eyes. "Don't even think about it."

"What?" Tamara looked at her innocently.

"Tamara, I know both of us are in the same place when it comes to wanting to connect with some man who will mean something in our lives. But trust me, Clay is not the man for you."

Tamara laughed. "I just asked a simple question," she protested.

"Well, I'm just warning you, simple question or

not, Clay is the worst bet for a relationship in the entire United States. He's moody and downright surly at times. He's a loner who is married to his work.''

"Stop! Stop!'' Tamara held up her hands and laughed once again. "All I asked was his age.''

"You also said he was handsome.''

"Well, I'd have to be dead not to notice that,'' she replied. "Trust me, Alyssa, I've heard enough about Clay from his mother to know he's not the man for me.''

What she didn't tell her friend was that even knowing Clay wasn't what she was looking for in a spirit mate, he intrigued her.

There was a dark intensity in his eyes that spoke of pain, a taut energy that whispered of a restless soul, and coupled with his passion for his work, she couldn't help but find him interesting.

He'd be fascinating to paint with his chiseled, strong, slightly arrogant features, although she usually didn't paint portraits.

"Hello?''

Alyssa's voice pulled her from her thoughts. "I'm sorry, what did you say?''

"I said what are your plans for the weekend?''

"Painting,'' Tamara replied. "The art gallery in Oklahoma City is giving me a show in September and I want to have at least five more paintings done by then. I'd ask you what you're going to do for the weekend, but I know your answer already. Work… work…work.''

"I like keeping busy,'' Alyssa said defensively.

"You going to tell me about the visions that have been bothering you lately?''

"I just have a few minutes before I need to get

back to the Redbud, I hate to end our visit with talking about them.''

Tamara reached across the table and took her friend's hand in hers. ''You can't carry it alone, Alyssa. Don't you realize that's what friends are for, to share not only joys, but burdens as well.''

Alyssa squeezed her hand, then released it and leaned back in the booth. ''I've had one vision that has become more and more frequent in the last two weeks and it's driving me crazy because I don't know where it's coming from.''

Tamara smiled at her. ''Might I remind you that you never know where they come from.''

Alyssa flashed a quick grin. ''Okay, that might be true, but this one feels different…more vivid…more intense…more powerful.'' She leaned forward once again, her gaze troubled. ''I see a man, one of the most handsome men I've ever seen…dark hair, eyes like blue ice and a smile that could melt a glacier on a winter day.''

''Have you ever seen him before? I mean, outside of your visions?''

Alyssa shook her head. ''Trust me, if I'd seen him outside a vision, I'd remember him. Anyway, in the vision, he's making love to me and then he's being stabbed and he's dying in my arms.'' She shuddered and took a sip of her iced tea. ''Anyway, this is one of the worst I've had in a long time and it always bothers me when they're recurring.''

''But you've had recurring visions that never came to anything before, right?'' Tamara asked.

''Right,'' Alyssa said after a moment of hesitation. ''Enough about this. Walk me home and I'll give you a double-dip cone on the house. I got in some of that caramel toffee ice cream that you love.''

''You've got a deal.'' Together the two women got up from the booth.

It was almost an hour later when Tamara got into her car and headed home. Her heart was warmed by the time she had spent with Alyssa. She'd love to have a special man in her life, but special friends were important, too.

As she drove down Main Street at a leisurely pace, her senses took in the sights and sounds that were so familiar to her.

When she'd been growing up her family had lived twenty miles outside of Cherokee Corners. Every Saturday her parents and she would get into the car and drive to town for grocery shopping, art supplies and whatever else the family might need.

She'd loved coming into town. Even though through the week she rode a bus to and from the Cherokee Corners schools, those Saturday trips of leisure time in Cherokee Corners had been magical.

It had only been since her return to Cherokee Corners from New York that she'd begun some volunteer work at the Cherokee Cultural Center. There she had met Alyssa and her Aunt Rita, Clay's mother.

Clay. There was absolutely no reason for him to be in her thoughts as much as he had been throughout the day. She had no explanation for it.

Since she'd returned from New York she had immersed herself in Cherokee ways and traditions, reclaiming the soul she'd nearly lost to Max and New York.

Eventually when she chose the man she would

marry, he'd be a warrior, proud of his heritage, strong in tradition and with the Cherokee loving heart.

Everything she had heard about Clay James indicated he was not the warrior her heart sought. She resolutely shoved thoughts of him out of her mind and focused on the fact that she had two lovely weekend days ahead of her to indulge in her first love… painting.

Thanks to Max, she no longer had to beg art galleries to showcase her work, rather she had galleries requesting showings.

She tucked away every penny she made, knowing that Native American paintings were hot now, but there may come a day when she wouldn't be able to give her work away.

Her parents had encouraged her talent and creativity from a very early age, but they had also instilled a level of practicality, which is why she had gotten her teaching degree despite the fact that painting was her first love.

She pulled down the dirt lane that would take her to her cottage, a sense of homecoming filling her up inside. The moment she'd seen the place, she'd thought of it as her own little enchanted cottage in the woods.

She'd known instinctively that it was a place where her creativity would thrive. The woods held a primal serenity that seemed to wrap her in its arms.

As she approached the cottage, she frowned. There was something on her porch…something that didn't belong there. She shut off her engine and sat for a long moment, trying to identify the dark bulk that was right in front of her front door.

Whatever it was, it wasn't moving. She got out of

the car, feeling a bit unsteady on her feet as she approached the porch.

A deer. A doe, actually. Lifeless, with soft brown eyes staring toward the heavens, it looked pitifully small.

Tamara sent up a prayer for the soul of the doe, at the same time wondering how it had gotten on her front porch. Had it been hit by a car and somehow stumbled here, broken and bleeding?

She bent down to get a better look, to try to discern what injuries the poor thing had sustained. Her blood chilled as she saw the claw marks that marred the tan hide of the doe's side. The claw marks looked like the ones that had marked her classroom walls. What was going on?

Fear walked up her backbone with icy fingers as she looked around. The surrounding woods was beginning to take on the shadows of twilight, creating dark pockets of shadows that she recognized would make perfect hiding places.

With trembling fingers, she unlocked her front door and stepped over the dead deer. She stood in the threshold of her home, listening for a sound that didn't belong, smelling the air for an alien scent, needing to be sure the sanctity of her home hadn't been breached before she entered farther.

She heard nothing, smelled nothing, but was spooked beyond belief. She hurried across the living room, grabbed her cordless phone and punched in 911.

Chapter 4

Clay had just left the lab and entered the police station when he heard Jason Sheller grumbling about having to go out to the Greystone residence because she'd found a dead animal on her property.

"She lives out in the woods, for crying out loud," Jason complained. "There's always dead animals out in the woods."

"I'll take it for you," Clay said.

Jason looked at him in mock surprise. "Ah, I forgot you lab rats were actually real cops who could take a report."

Clay eyed Jason with narrowed eyes. He'd never liked the man. He found him arrogant, self-centered and obnoxious. "You call me a lab rat again and I'll do an experiment on your face with my fists."

"Geez, lighten up, James." Jason backed up with hands in the air, the smug smirk that had crossed his mouth vanished. "It was just a little joke."

"I don't find your humor amusing," Clay replied. "Now, do you want me to take the call or not?"

"Sure, knock yourself out," Jason replied. He sank down at his desk. "Anything new on our slasher murders?"

"No." Clay gave his reports to the chief, not to individual officers. Glen would let the officers know what they needed to know when they needed to know it.

Besides, Clay was eager to get to Tamara's place and find out what was going on. She hadn't struck him as the type of woman who would freak out over some critter dying on her property.

Contrary to Jason Sheller's smart-ass remark, Clay and his team often worked as regular officers, filling in whenever necessary.

In a town the size of Cherokee Corners and with their limited equipment, there wasn't enough forensic work to keep the CSI team busy all the time.

He got into the van and took off for Tamara's place, his thoughts racing as he drove. After eating dinner with her and Alyssa, he'd gone back to the lab and had tried to make sense of the customer lists from quarries and landscaping services that had begun to come in.

Most of the places had simply printed off customer lists without pulling the ones Clay was specifically looking for. He now knew the decorative rock he'd found both at his parents' home and at the Frazier murder scene was called Dalmatian mix because of the unusual black and white coloring. Thankfully it was a high-end decorative rock, so not many people sprang for it.

From the lists he'd received so far he had a list of

fifty-two names from Oklahoma City and its surrounding area. Who knew how many more names
would be added when all was said and done.

And even then, being armed with a list of every
person in Oklahoma who'd ever bought the Dalmatian mix didn't mean he had the name of the person
who had killed at least two people and stolen his
mother away. For all he knew the killer could be from
Texas, or Kansas, or forty-seven other states.

As he turned down the dirt road that led to Tamara's cottage, he tried to put it all out of his head.
Instead his thoughts were replaced with the memory
of Alyssa telling him about the vision she'd suffered
the night before, the vision of Tamara being killed by
a monster.

He knew his cousin had been particularly fragile
over the last couple of months. Before the crime at
his parents' house Alyssa had been experiencing what
she said were the worst visions she'd ever had. She'd
told him all she saw was blackness, but accompany-
ing the dark was an overwhelming feeling that something terrible was going to happen.

Since the crime, Clay knew she blamed herself for
not "seeing" exactly what was going to happen, for
not "seeing" clues that would lead to the recovery
of Rita wherever she was.

Alyssa was fragile and under stress, and he was
certain that hearing about the damage to Tamara's
classroom was what had prompted her latest vision.

Twilight was on its way out the door, leaving behind the deep shadows of night. It would be even
darker around Tamara's place where the woods were
thick and kept out most of the moonlight.

As the cottage came into view, he saw that there

were no lights on. It looked as if nobody was home. He parked next to her car, then saw her seated behind the steering wheel.

She got out as he did. "Clay," she said with obvious surprise. "I didn't expect to see you."

"Since I was out at the schoolhouse, I decided to go ahead and come out here and take a report." She looked tense...frightened. "Is there a reason you're out here sitting in your car instead of inside?"

"I wasn't sure it was safe inside. I know it sounds silly, but I got spooked and just stepped in long enough to grab the phone and call the police, then I came out here, started the car engine and locked myself inside."

"It doesn't sound silly, it sounds like the intelligent thing to do." He leaned into the van and removed his handgun from the seat. "So, what exactly have we got here?"

"There's a dead deer on my porch." Her voice was low and steady. "At first I thought maybe it had been hit by a car and had somehow made its way to the porch, but when I looked more closely at it, I realized there were claw marks across its side like the ones that were made in my classroom. That's when I got spooked."

"Lock yourself back in the car and let me check out the house. Once it's clear, then I'll take a look at the deer."

He was glad she didn't question or argue with him, but instead did exactly what he asked.

When she was back in her car, he released the safety on his gun and approached the cottage. There were no lights on, but he could see just enough to step over the dead animal and push open the front door.

Gun firmly gripped in his hand and held up before him, he stepped through the door and flipped on the light switches that illuminated both the porch and the lamps on the end tables in the living room.

The room looked exactly as it had last night when he had been inside. Nothing appeared to be out of place, but he wouldn't be at ease until he'd checked every room, every closet, every place that a person might hide.

From the living room he moved into the kitchen, hitting the switch to light the room. Again, everything looked normal. He checked the small pantry, finding nothing more than canned goods, then left the kitchen and moved down the narrow hallway. The bathroom was tiny and the shower curtain hid nothing more than a spotlessly clean tub.

At the end of the hallway was the single bedroom. Clay turned on the light switch, tensed and ready for confrontation. Again he found nothing…except a bedroom that instantly assailed him on all senses, evoking thoughts that definitely had nothing to do with his job.

A bright red spread covered the double bed. Sprawled across the bed was a splash of yellow silk that he recognized must be Tamara's nightgown. Yellow and red curtains hung at the single window the room boasted, a window unit air conditioner filling the lower portion of the window itself.

The room breathed color and life and passion and it smelled like her…that mysterious blend of wildflowers and fresh rain and dark woods.

Dream catchers hung on the wall above the bed and

Tamara's artwork—rich, bold and intense in stroke, color and content—decorated the remaining walls. A tabletop fountain sat in the center of the dresser and it was easy to imagine making love to the sound of the gentle, bubbling water.

He yanked open the closet door, irritated that the thought of making love in this room, to the woman outside sitting in her car, had even entered his mind.

There was nothing in the house to indicate that somebody had been inside other than Tamara. He returned to the front door, stepped over the deer, then went to her car. Before he could reach it, she stepped out.

"Everything looks okay inside," he said. "And now I want to take a look at that deer." He went back to his van and pulled out his kit, then carried it back to the front porch.

He was intensely aware of her just behind him, could hear the whisper of her footsteps in the grass, could smell the faint pleasant fragrance that seemed to wrap around her.

It irritated him, making it difficult for him to focus on the task at hand. "You go on inside. I'll let you know when I'm finished here."

His voice was sharper than he intended, but it served his purpose. She stepped over the deer and disappeared into the house, silently closing the door behind her.

Clay pulled on latex gloves and got to work. At first glance it appeared as if vicious claws had ripped the deer, but it didn't take long for him to discover that the cause of death had been a bullet in the chest. The claw marks had been made postmortem.

He took photos of the dead animal, then carefully

measured the claw marks and took notes so he could find out if they matched the ones from the classroom.

It was difficult to discern when the deer had died, but it had been some time in the last twenty-four hours. He frowned and stood as he ripped off his gloves. Somebody had killed a deer with a bullet, then carried it here, to Tamara's porch, then had scored the hide with some sort of claws. Why?

He knocked twice on her door then pushed it open and entered the cottage. She wasn't in the living room, but he found her seated at the table in the kitchen, a cup of coffee in front of her.

She rose as he entered the room and went to the cabinet to retrieve another cup. She poured the coffee, then handed it to him.

"Thanks," he said and sat at the table. She returned to her chair across from him and gazed at him expectantly. "You've got a dead deer on the porch."

She smiled. "I didn't need a police officer to tell me that."

"The deer wasn't killed by being torn apart by claws, it was killed with a bullet."

"A bullet?" She looked at him in surprise. "A hunter? But why would he put the deer on my front porch? And what about those marks on the deer's side?"

She still wore the yellow dress that she'd had on when they'd had lunch, and he instantly thought of the yellow silk nightgown he'd seen splashed across the red of her bed.

He could almost envision that tiny piece of silk against her skin, the length of her long legs beneath the short nightie. He mentally shook himself, trying to remove the image of her wearing that little piece of silk.

"I think we need to consider that the deer and the vandalism in your classroom are tied together."

"Because of the claw marks," she said.

He nodded. "They appear to be the same kind of marks, either cougar or possibly a small bear. What I don't understand is why the deer was left here... possibly to frighten you?"

"Or perhaps as an offering." She said the words as if she had some sort of secret knowledge.

"An offering?" He gazed at her curiously. "What do you mean?"

She sighed, the sound like the wearied wind through the tops of the trees. "I think it's possible that this is all some sort of crazy joke."

He leaned back in the chair and eyed her intently. "Then you'd better tell me what the joke is because I'm not finding anything about this funny."

Tamara stood. "Let's go into the living room where it's more comfortable, then I'll explain." She grabbed her coffee cup and gestured for him to do the same.

She was intensely aware of him just behind her as she went into the living room. It had been a shock to see him. She'd expected an officer, but she hadn't expected Clay.

When those dark eyes of his focused on her so intently, it was difficult for her to concentrate. She was again aware of the hint of something dangerous, yet delicious, simmering just beneath his surface.

Her kitchen table had been too small to sit opposite him. She needed some space between herself and him.

In the living room she sat on the chair, leaving the sofa to him. She didn't speak until he'd sank down onto the cushion, his cup of coffee in hand.

"I think it's very possible that one of my students is playing a prank of sorts," she said.

"The destruction in your classroom goes beyond a simple prank." He leaned forward and set his coffee on a coaster on the coffee table.

"Yes, but if it is one of my students, you have to remember they're teenagers and sometimes they don't have a handle on the area of boundaries."

"What makes you think this might be the work of one of your students?"

She leaned back in her chair, hoping the additional inches of distance from him would make her focus on the conversation at hand. She tried not to focus on the length of his dark lashes, the broadness of his chest, and the scent that clung to him that reminded her of an untamed forest coupled with the bold scent of clean male.

"Part of what I teach my students are Native legends, like how the Milky Way came to be, why the opossum's tail is bare, how the earth got fire. You know, the kinds of legends we grew up on. Anyway, the past week, I've been teaching a more obscure legend…the legend of the bear."

"Legend of the bear?" He frowned thoughtfully. "I'm not sure I'm familiar with that one."

"There are several legends involving bears, but this particular one is about a lovesick bear. One day in the forest the bear sees a lovely Native maiden and he falls in love with her. For the next two full moons, the bear wreaks havoc on the village, killing their animals, terrorizing their children and scoring the trees that surrounded the area.''

"And so the moral of this story is love makes men savage beasts?'' Clay asked dryly.

Tamara smiled. "No, that isn't the moral of the story. You have to hear the rest of it before you realize the moral.''

"Then please continue,'' he said.

She nodded. "Finally the bear gets the maiden alone and he tells her of his love for her, that for the past two moons he's been showing her his strength, his prowess. He tells her he wants to claim her as his mate, but the Native maiden tells him no, that bears are quick to anger and savage when roused. The bear assures her that he can overcome these innate characteristics, that with her he will be as gentle as a lamb, as good-natured as a rabbit. Still, the maiden said no and the bear got so angry he killed the maiden. As she is dying she asks him why and he tells her that despite his intentions to the contrary, it's his nature.''

"And so the moral of the story is you can't change the nature of the beast.''

"You can't change the nature of anything. We are what we are.'' She averted her gaze from Clay and stared at one of her own paintings on the wall just behind him. It was about the legend of the bear come alive, in vivid colors and broad strokes. The painting showed a bear hiding behind a tree, watching a Native maiden washing in a stream. "It would be a stretch of coincidence not to think that my teaching that particular legend in the past week and these two incidences happening now are related.''

"I think you're right, it's got to be related,'' he agreed. His onyx eyes gave **nothing away** as he reached into his pocket and drew out a pad and pen. "I assume you provided the officers at the scene at the school a list of the names of your students?" She nodded.

"Well, now let's talk about what students you think might be capable of all this."

"I can't imagine any of them doing these things," she replied.

"You're going to have to do better than that, Tamara."

She liked the way her name sounded falling from his lips, like a swatch of silk being drawn across soft skin. But the look on his face was anything but silky. He wanted answers and it was clear from his facial expression that he was short on patience.

"Just tell me the first names that pop into your head when you think of potential suspects. I'd like to get this whole mess cleared up as soon as possible."

"And I assure you my only goal is to help you do just that," she replied with a calmness that was in direct contrast to his sharp tone.

He leaned back in the chair and reached for his coffee cup. He sipped his coffee, his dark gaze not leaving hers. "I'm sorry if I seem brusque or impatient. I've got a lot on my plate at the moment and the last thing this town needs is some crazed teenager acting like an enraged bear."

She realized then that what she'd thought were brackets of grimness around his mouth was probably exhaustion. "Terry Black. He's a difficult student, a bully with a bad temper and comes from a very dysfunctional family."

Clay wrote the name down in his pad, then looked at her again expectantly. She frowned thoughtfully, thinking of the students she taught in the summer school classes and the adults she taught at night.

She rubbed her hand across her forehead, once again staring at the painting just above where Clay sat. "There's also Benjamin Smith, he's in my adult class and I'm not sure why he's taking the class. He's a jerk and doesn't seem to be the least bit interested in Native American culture, but he shows up for class every Tuesday and Thursday night."

"Has he ever shown a personal interest in you?"

"Benjamin Smith shows an interest in anyone who is female. He fancies himself something of a ladies' man and he's good-looking enough, but he's so obnoxious that it plays against him."

Again he wrote the name down, then looked back at her. "Anyone else that sets off any kind of warning bells?"

She frowned thoughtfully. "Not off the top of my head, but let me think for a moment." She stood and grabbed her coffee cup. "I'm going to freshen up my coffee, would you like some more?"

"No, I'm fine."

She escaped into the kitchen, her thoughts in turmoil. She didn't want to believe that one of her students was capable of vandalism and the senseless death of an innocent deer, but she had to face the reality that it was the only thing that made a horrible kind of sense.

It wasn't just the pain of recognizing that somebody close to her was capable of terrible things, it was also Clay that had her stomach tied in knots.

No matter how tightly he pressed his sensual lips together, she wondered what they'd feel like against her own. No matter how tense he held his shoulders, she wondered if the flesh that covered those taut muscles would be warm and firm beneath her fingertips?

He made her aware of herself as a female. When those black eyes of his held her gaze she felt a tightening in her nipples, a liquid warmth sweep though her as her pulse raced just a little too quickly.

Instead of refilling her coffee cup, she got a glass of ice and filled it with water. Maybe the iced liquid would stop the heat that seemed to suffuse her body. Maybe the chill of the drink would halt the physical reaction she felt whenever he was near.

When she returned to the living room he stood looking at the painting on the wall that had drawn her attention earlier.

He turned as she approached. "The legend of the bear," he observed.

"The legend intrigues me on several different levels," she explained. "Which is one of the reasons I teach it."

"What do you find intriguing about it?" He stood in front of the chair where she had been sitting, far too close to where she stood.

She stepped backward and sat on the sofa, relieved to have just a little bit of distance from him. "I teach the legend because too many young women fall in love with men they think they can change and vice versa. I teach the legend to make the students realize that the nature of the beast can rarely be changed."

"And what beast did you try to change?" Once again those dark eyes of his held her captive, making it difficult for her to draw breath. He moved across the room and sat next to her on the sofa, close enough that he was invading her personal space.

"It wasn't a beast I tried to change. It was a beast

who tried to change me, and we're getting way off the subject here,'' she protested.

There were some areas of her past life that were far too personal to share with a man who was merely investigating disturbing incidents in her present life. ''And I have another name for you to add to the list.''

He pulled the notepad and pen from his pocket once again. ''Who?''

''Charlie Tamer. He's seventeen, a good student but with some emotional problems. I think he's on some medication for bipolar disorder. Perhaps he's stopped taking his medication recently.''

''I'll check him out. I'll check them all out, and I'll call Jeb Tanner to remove the deer from your porch as soon as possible.''

''Thank you, I appreciate it.'' Again she noted the lines of exhaustion that seemed to have taken possession of his handsome features. Even though she knew it would be dangerous, she had a sudden desire to stroke her hand down the side of his face, run her fingers across his creased brow.

All business between them appeared to be at an end, but he seemed in no hurry to leave. ''Now, I'd take a refill on the coffee,'' he said and leaned back into the sofa cushion.

''Sure,'' she said in surprise. She set her water on the coffee table and picked up his coffee cup, then returned to the kitchen.

A moment later she returned with his coffee. Again he surprised her by patting the sofa next to him. ''Please.'' He took the coffee from her, then she sat on the other side of the sofa, wondering what he was thinking and why he was still here.

"So, tell me again why I don't remember ever seeing you in town when we were growing up."

"My parents and I lived on a small farm about twenty miles outside of Cherokee Corners. When I was a child I came into town for school, then back home again. By the time I was a teenager and could drive, there wasn't much point in my coming into town except for something I'd need to buy."

"No Friday night hang with the girls, or cheerleading practices?"

Tamara laughed. "Definitely not. I wasn't the cheerleading type." Her smile faded as she thought of those teenage days. "As to hanging out with the girls, you have to understand something about girls. Friendships and cliques are usually formed in junior high, and during my junior high school days I wasn't in town much."

"So, you missed out on being part of a clique?"

She smiled. "Unless you consider being a nerd as a clique."

He raised a dark eyebrow and one corner of his lips curved upward. "I thought I was the only nerd in high school."

She laughed again, this time in disbelief. "I can't think of anyone less like a nerd than you."

"It's true." He paused a moment to take a sip of his coffee, then continued. "Like you I didn't do any of the school activities, didn't belong to any clubs or play sports."

She leaned toward him, intrigued by the glimpse of a younger Clay. "Why not?"

She would have thought it impossible for his eyes to grow darker, but they did. "I already knew what interested me and it had nothing to do with clubs or sports.''

She nodded in understanding. ''It was the same for me. Art was everything to me, but my parents made me realize that if an art career didn't pan out I needed something else to fall back on, something to pay the bills. I decided to get my teaching degree, but knew my parents didn't have the money to send me to college, so I started working at an early age to make sure my grades were good enough for a full scholarship somewhere. I was the studious weirdo who always had a sketch pad in my hand.''

''Surely a sketch pad didn't scare away the local boys,'' he observed, a new light in his eyes. His gaze swept over her, creating heat where it stopped and lingered. ''I mean, you're an attractive woman.''

''Thank you for the compliment,'' she said, surprised to discover her voice slightly shaky. That light in his eyes seemed to hold the warmth of the sun. ''I didn't take the time for boys when I was in high school or college. I was completely focused on my work.'' She'd waited for the right man...Mr. Wrong, Mr. Smooth-talking, Max Bishop.

''According to my sisters, that isn't focused, that's obsessed,'' he replied dryly.

''Yes, I've heard that term used where you're concerned,'' she said.

''So, I guess in that respect we're two birds of a feather,'' he observed.

His eyes still held a light that seemed to glitter and shine inside her. Dangerous. The man was positively lethal, she thought. She stood.

''Clay, it's getting late and I've had a long day. Is there anything else you need to know?''

He set his cup down and stood as well. "Actually, there is." She looked at him expectantly.

"I was wondering if perhaps you'd like to have dinner with me tomorrow night."

Shock swept through her. A dinner invitation was the last thing she'd expected from him. Accepting would be the height of stupidity. He was nothing like what she needed, what she wanted in her life. "Dinner sounds nice," she was appalled to hear herself say.

"Good." They walked together to the front door, then he turned back to face her. "Why don't I pick you up about six."

Stop it now, her brain screamed. Just say you've changed you mind. "Six sounds perfect."

The gleam in his eyes seemed to intensify and she felt as if the ground beneath her feet was shaking slightly. "Then I'll see you tomorrow at six."

Before she knew his intention, he leaned forward and placed his lips against hers. He touched her in no other way, but the feel of his warm mouth shot fire through her entire body.

He didn't attempt to deepen the kiss, but rather stepped back abruptly as if the intimate contact had surprised him as much as it had her. "Good night, Tamara." Without waiting for any reply from her, he disappeared out her front door.

She shut the door behind him and carefully locked it, surprised to see that her fingers trembled slightly. With the simple touch of his lips against hers, he'd sent a volcanic wave of heat through her. He'd made her feel needy and vulnerable, but more frightening and exciting than that, he'd made her hunger for more.

Chapter 5

A distraction. He was in desperate need of a distraction and what better to serve the purpose than an intelligent woman who exuded sensuality.

A desperate need for distraction was the only way to explain what had happened last night at Tamara's place.

He'd felt it again last night the moment he'd walked through her door—a calm peacefulness that he'd found oddly soothing. It had been like walking from the middle of a busy highway into a lush, quiet garden. He didn't know if it was the surroundings or the woman that created the mood of tranquility.

He took a bite of his sandwich and stared out the single window the small lab possessed. It was just after noon and the heat outside shimmered in the air, bouncing off the pavement and reflecting off a nearby tin roof.

Heat. It was what he'd felt every time his gaze had

met hers the night before. Heat—it was what had prompted him to issue a dinner invitation and what had led to that kiss that had shaken him to his very core.

The kiss had kept him up half the night. Even though it had been brief, nearly over even as it had begun, it had stirred his senses into overload.

In that brief mouth-to-mouth contact with her he'd wanted to tangle his hands in the length of her hair, lay her down on the plush throw rug beneath their feet and drag his mouth over every inch of her body.

In that split second of tasting her lips his blood had pumped rich and hot throughout his body. He couldn't ever remember such an instantaneous, physical reaction to a simple kiss before.

Even now as he thought of that tiny piece of yellow silk he'd seen on her bed, the heat from the outside seemed to crawl inside him. Yes, she would make the perfect distraction...at least for a little while.

"Is this what we pay our tax dollars for...to let our law enforcement officers sit and daydream out the window?"

The deep, familiar voice brought a smile to Clay's mouth as he turned to see the slightly stout, dapper gentleman standing in the doorway.

"Jacob, what brings you to the lab? Did I forget to make a mortgage payment?" He gestured to the chair across from his desk.

"Ah, I never have to worry about the James family making their payments on time." Jacob eased into the chair and patted the top his head, as if to assure himself that every one of his short gray hairs were in place. "What I am worried about is you."

"Me?" Clay looked at him in surprise.

"My sources tell me you're working far too many hours."

"I am," Clay agreed. "But, until we find Mom and we've got the person who is stabbing men and leaving them naked in the street behind bars, I'm probably going to be working too many hours."

"I've missed you dropping in for coffee."

Affection for the older man welled up in Clay. Jacob Kincaid, the only banker and the wealthiest man in town, had been a close friend of his parents, but he and Clay had always enjoyed a bond of friendship.

"I thought about it the other day, that it had been too long since I'd dropped in to visit with you, but then I got busy with things."

"I stopped by to see your dad earlier this morning," Jacob said. "He seems to be having a difficult time of it."

"Uncle Sammy isn't much of a substitute for Mom."

"Your uncle Sammy isn't a very good substitute for a man," Jacob said, then grimaced. "Sorry, I shouldn't have said that."

"No need to apologize for speaking the truth." Clay leaned back in his chair and thought about his uncle Sammy. Sammy James was Clay's father Thomas's baby brother.

Sammy's past had been checkered, although he'd been a favorite relative of the James siblings. Throughout their childhood, Sammy had flown in and out of Cherokee Corners like a turbulent summer storm. He'd changed addresses like other people changed clothes. His family never knew for sure where he'd been before a visit or where he was headed when he left. When he was around there was always excitement and laughter.

But more than once, Clay had heard Sammy and his dad fighting. Thomas had often told his brother to grow up, take responsibility for his life, to stop being a leech.

Still, he was glad that Sammy had come to help take care of Clay's father, leaving Clay and his sisters to spend most of their time and attention on trying to find their mother and the person who was responsible for the crime.

"Anything new?" Jacob asked.

Clay knew Jacob was asking about his parents' case. Nobody except Clay, his sisters, and Glen knew about the decorative rock found at the scenes, and nobody else knew about the strong tie to the Frazier case in Sycamore Heights and a third case in Sequoia Falls.

Although Clay trusted Jacob, he knew the more people who knew about the elements of the case, the more difficult it might become to catch a culprit. "No, nothing knew," he replied.

"Do you think it would help if I upped the reward money?"

"No, I appreciate the offer, but I don't think it would help. In fact, it would probably simply complicate things. For the first week or two after you put up the reward, we got nothing but false leads and crank calls, people sniffing after the money with nothing to give us. Upping the reward will just result in another flurry of useless phone calls."

Jacob nodded, then sighed. "I just feel so helpless. Even your father won't let me do anything to help him."

"He's a proud man. All he wants is Mom back home, and unless you can accomplish that, there's nothing you can do to help him."

"What about you?" Jacob leaned forward, his pale blue eyes holding warm concern. The scent of expensive cologne wafted from him. "What can I do to help you?"

Clay laughed, the sound a grim bark that had nothing to do with humor. "You can find my mother, catch the serial killer and find out who's decided to terrorize our local artist."

One of Jacob's gray eyebrows lifted slightly. "Tamara Greystone?"

Clay nodded, surprised that even the sound of her name pulled forth the memory of the sweet taste of her lips. "Somebody trashed her classroom at the school, then last night a dead, mutilated deer was left on her front porch."

"Kids?"

"Probably. We're checking it all out now."

"Beautiful young woman," Jacob observed. "And quite talented. I own several of her early pieces. At the time I bought them I knew she'd be going places in the art world."

Clay smiled wryly. "You own several pieces of everyone's work."

Jacob smiled, lifting the jowls that had begun to form in recent years. "That reminds me, I just acquired a new bronze that you must come and see. It's absolutely stunning and is a beautiful addition to my collection."

"You're obsessed, Jacob," Clay said affectionately. "If you happen to pass away at home, it will take us days to find your body in that mansion of yours amid all of your collections.''

''On that cheerful note, I think I'll take my leave.'' Jacob stood and Clay did as well. ''Let me know if there's anything I can do, Clay,'' Jacob said as they reached the door to the lab that led into the police station proper.

''Just keep visiting Dad. He needs his friends' support right now.''

''That goes without saying,'' Jacob agreed. The two men said their goodbyes then Clay returned to his desk, but instead of getting back to work, he stared out the window once again.

Anything new, Jacob had asked. How Clay wished they had a substantial lead to follow in the case of his mother's disappearance. The rock that he'd found might be important, or it might lead to nothing. The fingerprints in the house had all been identified as family and friends.

Trace evidence was still at the lab in Oklahoma City, a bigger lab with better equipment than what Clay possessed here. He was hoping something would be found there to point a finger to a likely suspect, but hope was getting more difficult to sustain with each passing day.

A distraction. In truth, that was probably the last thing he needed in his life at the moment. What he needed was more energy, more focus, more minutes in the day to find his mother. But she was such a fine distraction, a little voice whispered inside his head.

His gaze went from the window to the phone. Call and cancel. That was the smart thing to do. The last thing he needed was to go out to dinner with a woman he had nothing in common with, a woman who physically stirred him half-mindless.

The last woman he needed to get involved with in any way was Tamara Greystone, who taught Native legends he didn't believe in and adhered to old traditions he'd long ago eschewed.

Even knowing the smartest thing to do was cancel the dinner date, his hand didn't reach for the phone. It was already after two, and it would be rude to cancel at this late time.

No, he'd go ahead and take her to dinner. They had absolutely nothing in common and their only connection was the crime that had taken place in her classroom.

They'd probably suffer unendurable lengths of uncomfortable silences, followed by severe heartburn and both would come away from the meal knowing the idea of them sharing personal time together was nothing more than a bad idea.

It was ridiculous that it took her so much time to get dressed for a date she wasn't sure she wanted to keep. For the fourth time in as many minutes she pulled an outfit from her closet, then threw it on the bed.

It was five-thirty. She'd already had a long, luxurious bubble bath, washed and brushed her hair, put on a touch of makeup, but at this rate she'd be trying to pick a dress to wear as their dinner reservations were given to somebody else.

The problem was she wasn't sure if she wanted to dress to please herself or dress to please him. Even though she knew the dinner invitation had been spontaneous, prompted by who knew what, she still intended to have a nice evening.

She finally decided to dress to please herself. She'd spent enough time trying to please Max that now the idea of dressing for a man, being something other than what she was, left a bad taste in her mouth.

The tear dress she finally chose to wear was turquoise calico with an appliqué pattern of coral diamonds around the yoke and the bottom of the long skirt. Coral buttons adorned the dress from the neckline to the hem. She added coral earrings and sandals and pronounced herself ready.

As she stood in her living room, waiting for Clay to arrive, she realized that by choosing to wear a traditional Cherokee tear dress she was instantly placing a barrier between her and Clay.

She knew from spending time with Rita that, for some unknown reason, Clay had turned his back on the Cherokee ways and his Native American blood. He probably wouldn't be pleased to see her dressed in the traditional Cherokee clothing. But this was who she was and besides, it was only a meal they were sharing. She knew better than to expect or anticipate anything more.

At precisely six o'clock he pulled in front of her cottage. Instead of driving the white van she'd seen him in before, he drove a shiny dark blue two-door sports car.

She watched as he unfolded from the driver door, surprised to feel her heart race just a little bit faster. He was dressed in a pair of navy dress slacks and a short-sleeved pale blue shirt.

Even though she was peeking through the curtain at the window and watching him approach, she could tell that despite the civility of the dress clothing, there was a barely suppressed energy, a simmering sensuality that she recognized as both evocative and dangerous.

She moved away from the window as he knocked, a rapid staccato that resounded in the pit of her stomach. She had a feeling this was a bad idea...a very bad idea. She grabbed her purse, then opened the door to greet him.

His dark brows rose in surprise. "I don't think I've ever had a woman be ready when I've arrived on time to pick them up."

"You said six. I assumed you meant six," she replied as she stepped out on the porch and pulled her door closed behind her.

"I made reservations for six-thirty at Vitello's. I hope you like Italian," he said.

"Love it," she replied. He opened the passenger door and she slid into the luxurious leather interior. As he walked around the front of the car to the driver door, she tried not to watch him.

The inside of the car smelled good, an aromatic blend of rich leather and Clay's clean scent. As he opened the car door and slid in behind the wheel she steeled herself against any physical reaction she might have to his nearness.

He seemed disinclined to speak as he started the engine and pulled away from her cottage. Instead he punched a button on the console and the air filled with the sounds of a light rock radio station.

He was pulled tight into himself. It was obvious in the way his hands clenched the steering wheel, in the rigid set of his shoulders and the way his gaze remained focused on the road ahead.

"You know, we didn't have to do this," she said softly.

"Do what?"

"Do this. Do dinner together."

He turned and eyed her curiously. "Why, you don't want to?"

She smiled. "It just looks like you'd rather be anywhere than here at the moment."

His shoulders relaxed, as did his grip on the steering wheel. He reached out and lowered the volume on the radio. "Sorry, I didn't mean to give you that impression. I guess I've been working so hard for so long, I've forgotten about the civil pleasantries of socializing."

"Now, there's a real crime," she said.

"Maybe, although most of the time I find my work more satisfying than any socializing I do."

"Then maybe you've been socializing with the wrong people."

Again he flashed her a glance and this time his lips were curved upward in a devastating smile. "Maybe you're right. Cops and criminals aren't usually overly adept at small talk."

"Well, I just wanted to let you know that if you'd rather not do this, you can take me back home. I don't want you to be where you don't want to be."

He looked back at the road, his expression once again inscrutable. "I'm fine with where I am at the moment."

She settled back in the seat and looked out the window.

Cherokee Corners had almost a dozen drive-through eateries, four cafés and two more upscale restaurants. Vitello's was one of the two. Located on the north side of town, it was housed in a single story bleached brick building with a neon sign across the top.

"Ever eaten here before?" he asked as he pulled into an empty parking space.

"No. Most of the time when I grab a bite out it's at one of the cafés." She didn't want to tell him that she hadn't been out on a date since her return to Cherokee Corners from New York nearly two years earlier.

"I haven't eaten here before, either. Hopefully the food is good. I'm hungry, what about you?"

"Starving," she agreed.

Together they got out of the car and walked toward the doors to the restaurant. She was intensely aware of his hand at the small of her back as they entered the dim interior and walked to where the hostess stood.

Although she knew it was impossible, she could have sworn she could feel the heat of his hand against her bare skin. He held his hand there until they were led to their table, only then did he break the physical contact.

Their table was situated in a corner of the room, providing far more intimacy than they required. A rich red tablecloth covered the small table and a candle flickered its romantic light between the salt and pepper shakers in the center of the table.

"If the food is as bad as the cheesy music they're playing, we're in trouble," Clay said when they were settled in with menus before them.

Tamara laughed and opened her menu. The "cheesy music" was an Italian instrumental, the kind that seemed indigenous to Italian restaurants all over the United States.

"I don't know how good the food is, but if the crowd is any indication, it must be pretty good," she said.

"It's been my experience that most weekend nights nobody stays home in this town," he observed and closed his menu.

"There isn't a whole lot to do other than eat out in this town."

"Quite a different pace than New York. It must have taken some adjustment for you to return to such a small town after the big city."

Tamara closed her menu as well. "Actually, the bigger adjustment came when I left here and moved to New York. I never really made the adjustment. Everything there always seemed too fast, too frantic and too surreal for me."

"What made you move there?"

It was hard for her to concentrate and look at him at the same time. The flickering candlelight emphasized the angles and planes of his handsome face, giving him a slightly predatory look.

She looked down at her menu cover. "My work…and the agent who agreed to represent me. He thought it would be a good idea if I lived in New York. So, after several months of thinking it over, I decided to give it a try."

She looked up into his dark eyes where the candlelight seemed to turn his pupils silver. "New York just didn't work out for me. I'm happier, more centered here in Cherokee Corners."

At that moment the waitress arrived to take their orders. When she'd departed with their orders in hand, Tamara sought to change the topic of conversation from her to him.

"Your work must be fascinating," she said.

"If you like science, which I do."

Again their conversation was interrupted as the waitress returned with a bottle of red wine and poured them each a glass, then departed once again.

"What made you decide to go into crime-scene investigation?" she asked, refusing to allow any awkward silences to develop between them.

He leaned back in his chair and took a sip of his wine, looking more relaxed than he had since the moment he'd picked her up. "When I was working homicide several years ago, my father came to me and told me he wanted a crime-scene investigator unit here in town. At that time he was chief of police and knew that particular part of police work had always intrigued me."

"Because you like science."

He nodded. "With science there's no guesswork. You run the tests, you get results. There's no room for emotion or trying to guess if somebody is lying to you. You don't have to deal with the human element at all."

For her, his answer was quite telling of the kind of man he was, the kind of man who had worried his open, giving mother, the kind of man who Tamara should have no interest in whatsoever.

"How's your father holding up?" she asked, then raised her wineglass to take a sip.

"As well as can be expected. It's difficult on him…as it is on all of us." He leaned forward. "I assume Jeb got the deer off your porch last night?"

It was obvious he wanted a subject change, that he

wasn't about to share any of his feelings with her about the disappearance of his mother. Tamara was neither surprised nor offended. He owed her nothing of his feelings.

"It was gone when I woke up this morning," she replied. "Thank you for talking to Jeb about it."

"In this heat, it needed to be disposed of as soon as possible. Have you thought anymore about anyone who might be living your legend?"

She smiled. "It isn't *my* legend and no, I still can't imagine anyone crazy enough to reenact the legend."

Again their conversation was interrupted, this time with the arrival of their meals. Clay had ordered lasagna and she had ordered linguine with Alfredo sauce and fresh vegetables. Her stomach growled as the waitress set the plate in front of her.

"It looks good," she said.

"Mine looks better." He smiled and again she was struck by the powerful sexual appeal he possessed and seemed utterly unaware of.

For the next few minutes they were silent as they began to eat. The music might be cheesy, but the food was beyond compare and the ambiance of the restaurant itself was comfortable.

Even the silence between them wasn't a strained or uncomfortable one. It was only when they both reached for the breadbasket at the same time and their hands made physical contact that she felt tension spring to life inside her.

"Sorry," she said and quickly drew back her hand.

"No problem." He took a slice of the warm Italian loaf and buttered it, then handed it to her. This time when their fingers made contact she was ready for the jolt of electricity the mere touch created.

"Thanks." The good thing about her bronze complexion was that blushes were difficult to discern, but she felt the warmth of a blush sweep through her. What was it about this man that affected her so strongly, affected her on such a visceral level?

Once again they fell silent and focused on their meals. Tamara's linguine was delicious, but she found the man seated across from her detracting from her appetite.

"So, why are you teaching? I understand from my sources that your paintings are quite a hot commodity," he said, breaking the silence that had begun to grow too long to be comfortable.

"Painting is a very isolating kind of work. It's just me and my canvases. The time I spend painting is intense, all-consuming and exhausting. Teaching makes me interact with other people, keeps the balance in my life that is so important to my well-being." She hesitated a beat, then added. "You should try it some time."

"What? Teaching?"

It was obvious he was intentionally being obtuse. "I'm not even going to dignify that with a reply," she said dryly.

He laughed. It was the first time she'd heard his laughter and the sound, as smooth as whipped cream, as rich as hot cocoa, warmed her from the inside out. With laughter on his lips, his eyes lightened and tiny starbursts of wrinkles creased his skin, making him impossibly attractive.

"I suppose at some time or another my mother has told you that I'm not much into balance. Work is what counts with me and that pretty much sums up my life."

"And I suppose at some time or another your mother has told you that's not a healthy way to live."

The light that had momentarily illuminated his eyes was doused and his features grew taut. She'd obviously stepped on toes and brought up a painful subject. "But we each make the choices that are most comfortable for ourselves," she added, hoping to dispel the darkness that suddenly clung to him.

"Yeah, I suppose, and I guess you just hope that in making your choices you don't wind up hurting anyone else," he said.

She leaned forward, wishing to find the words to dispel the pall that had swept over him so suddenly. "But that's the basis of the Cherokee philosophy, to do no harm, to foster respect and harmony with the world and nature."

One of his dark brows rose as he gazed at her. "Are you lecturing me, Ms. Teacher?"

She was pleased to see a teasing light in his eyes. "Probably," she replied, then laughed. "And I apologize, I didn't mean to. It's second nature to me as a teacher."

"I guess it's like cops who interrogate rather than communicate." Once again he looked relaxed.

"Is that what you do? Interrogate rather than communicate?"

He smiled and reached for another slice of the bread. "According to my sisters I don't do either very well. I'm sure you've met my sisters, Breanna and Savannah."

"Yes, although I don't know them well. I did hear that Savannah might be leaving the police force."

"She's talking about transferring to the Sycamore Ridge Police Department. She's recently moved in with Riley Frazier and they're planning on getting married. But he's a home builder and lives in Sycamore Ridge.''

''When are they getting married?'' she asked, hoping the touch of wistfulness that swept through her wasn't evident in her voice.

''I'm not sure. I don't think they've made definite plans. And I just found out the other day that Breanna is pregnant.''

''Oh, isn't that wonderful. You're going to be an uncle.''

''I'm already an uncle. Breanna has a daughter, Maggie.'' A smile once again curved his sensual lips… a warmer, sweeter smile than she'd ever seen. It was obvious Maggie held a special place in his affections. ''And those two sisters of mine were the last women I expected to see married and happy.''

''Why is that?'' Tamara pushed her nearly empty plate to the side.

''They both had their hearts banged around pretty badly in the past. Breanna's first husband stayed in her life just long enough to get her pregnant with Maggie, then left her. Savannah's husband died when his car crashed and went into the Cherokee River. They were both pretty torn up for a long time, I figured they'd wind up old spinsters.''

''What about you? A broken heart in your past?'' she asked lightly.

The light in his eyes grew hard, glittering like silvery diamonds. ''Not me, never put my heart on the line where it had the potential of being broken. And never intend to, either.''

There was an unspoken warning in his words, in his eyes, but he needn't have bothered. She knew not to expect anything from Clay James, except the meal they had just shared. She wanted nothing more from him. She'd never again be a fool with her heart.

"How about some dessert?" he asked.

"Nothing for me," she replied. "I ate too much pasta and didn't leave room for dessert."

At that moment a faint ring sounded. Clay grabbed a small cellular phone from his breast pocket. "Excuse me," he murmured to her, then flipped the phone. "James," he said into the phone. "Where?" He set up straight in his chair, tension positively oozing from his pores. "What time?" He glanced at his wristwatch and frowned. "No…no…I'm on my way. I should just be able to make it."

He flipped the phone, returned it to his pocket and was half out of his chair before he looked at her as if startled to see her sitting across from him. "Look…something has come up. I've got to get to Shadow Hills before nine o'clock." It was obvious he was in a hurry and didn't know what to do with her.

"Shadow Hills? Where's that?" she asked as she rose from the table.

"It's an hour drive from here if I push the speed limit a bit."

"Then I guess we'd better get going," she said.

He hesitated a moment, as if contemplating his actions where she was concerned. She knew he was figuring how much time he'd lose in taking her back home then getting on the road to Shadow Hills. "You don't mind taking the ride with me? It's nothing dangerous."

''We're wasting time,'' she said.

With a curt nod, he threw bills on the table, then took her by the elbow and led her out of the restaurant.

Chapter 6

It was the first break they'd had on his parents' case and as Clay pointed his car toward the small town of Shadow Hills, he prayed that it was the break they'd all been waiting for.

He shot a surreptitious glance at Tamara. On the one hand he was grateful she'd agreed to come along, erasing the extra time he'd have had to spend to take her back to her place.

On the other hand, he found her nearness in the small confines of the sports car disturbing, just as he'd found the entire dinner experience disturbing.

The turquoise and coral dress and accessories did amazing things to her skin, enriching the bronze tones and making it look intimately touchable. Her scent hadn't been lost to the fragrance of garlic and tomato sauce in the restaurant. Rather, it had seemed to surround his chair, invade his pores.

More than anything, what he'd found disturbing

was how much he liked the way her smile lit up the gray of her eyes, how much he enjoyed talking to her, and how much he wanted to kiss those lips of hers again…and again.

"What's in Shadow Hills?" she asked, breaking the silence that had enveloped them since they'd gotten into the car.

"Lucky's Pawnshop," he replied.

"And what's at Lucky's Pawnshop?"

His fingers tightened around the steering wheel. "Hopefully a couple of pieces of my mother's jewelry and an identification of the person who pawned them."

"Oh, Clay." She reached over and placed her warm fingers around his forearm. "Maybe this is the beginning of a trail that will lead to her whereabouts."

"Let's hope," he said, grateful when she removed her fingers from his arm. An instantaneous fire had licked in his stomach, coupled with a tightening of his groin at her touch.

"When Mom first went missing, none of us thought to check on the jewelry she kept in a secret compartment in their bed headboard. None of the jewelry in her jewelry box on the dresser had been touched and in the aftermath of the crime, none of us thought about the other jewelry."

He was talking less to her and more to himself, trying to get his focus back on what was important rather than dwell on what it was about Tamara Greystone that had his brain confused and his body on full alert.

"Anyway, last week Savannah remembered about the jewelry hidden away in the headboard and she checked and was surprised to find it gone. We immediately sent out descriptions of the pieces to the pawnshops in the state, hoping that something like this would happen.''

''The pieces are distinctive enough that you'll know for sure if they're your mother's?''

He nodded. ''The jewelry that was missing was all custom-made pieces that my father had done by a particular jeweler. They were mostly turquoise and silver pieces, but very distinctive in design.''

''And do you think they were pawned with a legitimate form of identification?'' she asked.

He frowned. ''If they weren't, then Lucky is going to become extremely unLucky. If I find that the shop didn't adhere to the proper procedure for a pawn, I'll close the shop down.'' He heard the hardness in his tone, felt the sharp cutting edge of anticipated frustration crawling up his throat.

Pawnshops were always a crapshoot when it came to those that functioned within the law and those that functioned outside the law. He hoped to hell Lucky's was one of the good places that adhered to state laws and regulations, because if they weren't, then he'd have no lead to follow on his mother.

''Are you okay? Cool enough?'' he asked. ''Want the radio on?''

''Clay, you don't have to worry about me. I'm fine. If I get too warm, I'll tell you. If I want music, I'll ask for it. I know your mind must be racing with a million thoughts. You don't have to make small talk with me if you don't feel like it.''

Oddly enough, her words made him relax a bit. She was the most undemanding woman he'd ever met and that simply served to increase his attraction to her.

"Are you always this easy to get along with?" he asked.

"Of course not." Her voice held a teasing lilt. "You've just managed to catch me on two good days."

"Lucky me."

"Actually, as far as I'm concerned, there isn't much in this life that is important enough to fight about. I pick my battles, and I only fight the big ones."

"That's refreshing. In my line of work I see people who fight about everything, people who get beat up or even killed because somebody lost their temper." He felt her gaze on him and turned to see those gray depths studying him. "What?"

"I just realized how utterly grim your work must be. You've chosen a field where you see the aftermath of violence over and over again. You see the worst of human emotions. You see hatred and anger, twisted passion and jealousy, murder and avarice."

"That's true," he agreed.

"But Clay...do you ever give yourself an opportunity to see the other side of human emotions?"

"Of course I do," he said, a hint of sharpness back in his voice. The last thing he needed at the moment was Tamara Greystone giving him the same kind of lecture that his mother had given him on numerous occasions.

His mother. His thoughts raced once again. This had to be the break. This had to be the break they'd needed to find her.

As he stared out the windshield into the dark night ahead, he tried not to get his hope up, knowing how easily hope could be shattered, leaving behind a sick emptiness that burned and ached in the pit of the stomach.

He glanced at the clock on the dash. They were about fifteen miles from Shadow Hills and it was eight-forty. He knew the pawnshop closed at nine and if he didn't get there before then, the investigation might have to wait until morning.

Urgency forced his foot down harder on the gas pedal. He was grateful that Tamara said nothing for he wanted his thoughts clean and focused for the task to come.

Shadow Hills was so small it didn't even rate a dot on the maps. It boasted a large truck stop, a fried chicken drive-through, a post office, a grocery store and Lucky's Pawnshop.

Clay pulled to a halt in front of the large building where the lights were still on inside and the neon sign across the top flashed the Lucky name.

He and Tamara got out of the car and entered the shop to the accompaniment of a jingling bell hanging above the door. Clay took in the scenery in a quick scan. It was a typical pawn setup.

Shelves of stereo equipment, computers and miscellaneous electronic gadgets were on one side of the shop. Chain saws, lawn mowers and workout equipment were on the other side. At the back a counter stretched the width of the building. This would be where the jewelry for sale was displayed. The pieces were either sold outright to the store or were pawned and not retrieved within the usual ninety days.

Clay's adrenaline shot through him as he saw a video surveillance camera anchored on the wall up by the ceiling.

Behind the counter stood a middle-aged man who

was busily closing out the register. "If you want to do business, you'd better do it fast, I'm closing up for the night," he said without looking up.

Clay pulled out his wallet with his police badge and slammed it down on the counter. "I believe you called us."

The man looked up and raked a hand through his dirty blond hair. His blue eyes radiated a weary resignation. "Yeah, I called, but I didn't expect anyone to show up here tonight." He frowned with a touch of irritation. "Let me lock up, then we'll get to this business."

Clay fought a burst of impatience as the man walked around the counter and headed for the front door, keys jingling in his hand.

He looked at Tamara, who stood next to him. She was looking in the counter at the display of rings. There were cocktail rings, diamond wedding rings and fiery opals, all in either white or yellow gold settings.

"Just think," she said softly. "Each of these rings must have a story to tell."

"Yeah, probably stories of betrayal and heartache."

"Maybe some of them," she agreed, "but some of them might be stories of hope and happiness."

They fell silent as the man returned to the counter. He picked up Clay's identification and studied it for a minute. "Officer James, I'm Leonard Wilson, aka Lucky. I got the descriptions of the stolen items last week, but I wasn't working when they came in. I've been going over inventory today and realized we have a couple of pieces that might be what you're looking for."

It was obvious he intended to cooperate, and for that Clay was pleased. It would make things so much easier. Again he had to fight against the hope that buoyed inside him.

Maybe…finally…a break. "I hope you keep good records, demand proper identification when items are brought in for pawn or sale," Clay said.

Lucky nodded. "Look, I know pawnshops generally have a bad rap, but I run a clean business. I don't deal in guns or weapons of any kind, I don't knowingly take in stolen items and I keep impeccable records."

"Good, then we shouldn't have any problems." Clay returned his wallet with his badge and ID to his back pocket.

"I need to go into the back to get the items," Lucky said, and disappeared into a doorway that led to the back of the store.

Again Clay turned to Tamara. "See anything you like?" he asked, gesturing to the ring display she'd been studying.

She looked up at him and shook her head. "I'm not much into diamonds."

"I thought every woman loved diamonds."

She smiled, the warmth of the gesture lighting her gray eyes. "Not all women. I much prefer semiprecious to precious stones. Coral is my favorite." She touched one of the buttons of her dress, drawing his attention to the thrust of her breasts against the colorful material.

Despite the circumstances, in spite of their location, a wave of intense desire crashed into Clay and nearly buckled his knees. There was nothing he'd like more than to unfasten the buttons that held her dress together, shove aside the material and seek the warmth of her breasts in his hands, taste her sweet skin with his lips. God, but she was getting under his skin.

"Here we are," Lucky said as he returned to the counter with a large, sealed brown envelope.

Clay drew a deep breath to steady himself as the momentary burst of desire left him. He stared at the envelope on the counter, his fingers itching to rip it open and see if it contained his mother's items.

"These pieces were brought in for pawn last Thursday at two in the afternoon." He tore open the top of the envelope and spilled the contents on the counter.

Clay's heart leapt into his throat as he stared at the familiar items. There was a turquoise necklace, intricate in design and matching the bracelet next to it.

Clay remembered the last time he'd seen his mother wear the jewelry. She and his father had been on their way out to dinner and Rita had been a vision in a white sundress with the jewelry providing its colorful accents.

Anguish squeezed his heart, anguish that was quickly chased away by a sense of rage...that somebody had taken what belonged to Rita and brought them here, that somebody had taken Rita and had her someplace where she couldn't be found.

"Were they pawned or sold?" he asked, his voice sounding far away as anger roared in his head.

"Pawned. The guy who brought them in was given five hundred bucks for them."

Five hundred bucks. They were worth four times that amount. "And who brought them in?" Clay asked. He was vaguely aware of Tamara wrapping her fingers around his forearm, as if in an effort to offer support. He recognized that on some level, he appreciated the touch.

Lucky slid a sheet of paper in front of him. The paper was a photocopy of a valid driver's license. As Clay looked at the photo on the license, a loud roaring resounded in his brain as a startled gasp escaped him.

Staring back at him from the paper was a familiar face and for a moment he thought he might be hallucinating. But as he checked the name on the driver's license he knew he wasn't seeing things. The man who had brought in his mother's jewelry to pawn was Samuel James...Clay's Uncle Sammy.

Tamara heard his sharp intake of breath, felt the tension that rippled through him like a jolt of lightning striking his body. She didn't recognize the photo of the man on the paper, but she recognized the name and her heart ached for the pain and betrayal Clay must be feeling at this very moment.

She knew from local gossip that Sammy James, Clay's uncle, had come to town a couple of weeks ago to help take care of Thomas as he recuperated from the beating he'd received on the night his wife had disappeared.

Clay stood for a long moment staring at the photo, then looked up at Lucky. "You're certain this is the man who brought the items in."

Lucky nodded. "My partner wouldn't have taken them if the ID didn't match the man." He shoved the jewelry back into the brown envelope and sighed. "I suppose you'll need to take this with you. I guess I just eat the five hundred bucks."

"I'll write you a receipt and I'll see that you get your money," Clay said. Tamara withdrew her hand from his arm, noting the muscle that ticked dangerously in his jaw. She wouldn't want to be Samuel James right now for any amount of money in the world.

Within minutes she and Clay were again in his car and headed back to Cherokee Corners. He didn't say a word, but his anger filled the car. She made no attempt to alleviate or lessen his anger.

She didn't want to intrude in any way, knew that she'd been along for the ride only because of the circumstance that she'd been having dinner with him when the break had come in. She had no right to invade his emotions or intrude on his thoughts.

However, she couldn't help the fact that her heart hurt for him. She knew he'd been hoping for a clue…a lead to his mother and instead he'd discovered a family betrayal. She wished there were some way to take away his pain, but she also knew nothing she could do or say would touch the emotion that filled the car like a seething beast.

"There was a matching ring." He finally broke the silence. "It will probably show up sooner or later at some pawnshop nearby." Once again he fell silent as the car ate up the miles toward Cherokee Corners.

"Dammit." He slammed his hand against the steering wheel. Tamara jumped in response to his explosion. "The bastard! How could he have done something like this?"

The anger no longer simmered, but exploded out of him with each word. "How could he do this? Steal from us…from Mom. Didn't he think we'd find out? The stupid jerk didn't even go that far from home. What in the hell was he thinking?"

"He probably wasn't thinking," she said softly.

"People who do stupid things rarely think them through, nor do they consider the consequences of their actions."

"I'm going to show him consequences," Clay replied ominously. His fingers were so tight around the steering wheel she could see the white of his knuckles. "When I got the phone call, I'd hoped..." his voice trailed off and again Tamara's heart ached for him.

He didn't have to finish his sentence. She knew exactly what he'd hoped, that he'd get a name, a photograph or something that would lead him to the person who had his mother. He'd hoped and possibly prayed that this was a huge break in the case.

"He must have found the jewelry when he first arrived," he continued, his voice more steady than it had been moments before. "He must have found it before Savannah remembered to check on it and removed it from the compartment in the headboard."

Some of the anger that had wound him so tight, that had filled the interior of the car seemed to dissipate somewhat as he talked. "At least this proves one thing once and for all."

"What's that?" she asked.

"There's no way in hell my mother would have voluntarily left those pieces of jewelry behind. She had to have been taken from the house against her will."

Tamara looked at him in surprise. "Did anyone think otherwise?" She noticed that his hands had relaxed their grip on the steering wheel.

"Everyone had doubts, except my sisters and me. Even people who knew them well thought it was possible my mom and dad had had a fight and things had just gotten out of control. They thought mom had hit dad over the head, then packed a suitcase and ran.''

"How could anyone who knew Rita think such a thing?'' Indignation swept through her as she thought of the spirited, but loving Rita.

"You have to understand, even the people who know and love my mother also know that she and my father got into fights on occasion. And they often indulged in those fights in public. Add that to the fact that a suitcase was missing from Mom's closet, and some of her clothes and personal items were gone. Some people made what they thought was the logical assumption.''

"Your mother adores your father. Anyone who's seen them together can see the love that exists between them. It's ridiculous to think that she would have anything to do with harming your father.''

"My sentiments exactly,'' he said as he turned onto the dirt road that led to her cottage. "I'm sorry you got dragged into all this.''

"Nobody can tell me that a date with Clay James isn't an adventure,'' she teased.

"I appreciate you being a good sport about being dragged along.'' He pulled to a halt in front of her house. He turned to look at her and she saw the anger, although momentarily banked, still sizzling in the depths of his eyes.

"Clay…if you need to talk or just unwind or whatever, you know where I am.'' She wasn't sure what she was offering him, only knew that she couldn't get out of the car and go inside without offering something.

He studied her for a long moment, then reached out and touched the side of her face with his fingertips.

"You're a nice woman, Tamara. You'd be smart to keep away from me and my troubles." He dropped his hand from her face. "Good night."

"Good night, Clay." She got out of her car, her face still burning from his touch. Even though she knew she was a fool, his words of warning had only managed to draw her closer, made her want more from him. And that frightened her more than the vandalism in her classroom, more than the dead deer left on her porch.

Chapter 7

The rage that Clay had managed to control while Tamara was in the car exploded inside him the moment she got out. Mingling with the rage was a bitter burn of despair. He hadn't realized how high his hope had been that the pawnshop might yield a clue until now, with hope shattered.

The anger was easy to deal with, more familiar, and he allowed it to wrap around him and build inside him until it blocked out any other emotion.

He knew it would be wise to head home. It was quarter to eleven and his father would probably be in bed asleep. But he didn't head home. Rather, he drove in the direction of his mother and father's house. His father might be in bed, but Uncle Sammy was a late-nighter.

He'd still be up to face the consequences of his actions. All Clay had to figure out was what those consequences might be.

He could have Sammy arrested, but he didn't want his father to know how low his brother had fallen. Thomas was not only struggling with the weakness his injuries had left behind, he was also suffering from the loss of his beloved wife.

The last thing Clay wanted to do was add to his father's heartache. But he also wasn't willing to just let this ride. Uncle or not, Sammy had to know he'd stepped over a line and in the process had lost any respect Clay might have had for him.

What Clay really wanted to do was drive a fist through Sammy's face. He wanted to rant and scream, yell and curse at the man who would do such a thing as steal from his missing sister-in-law. Clay wanted Sammy to pay for raising his hopes, even for just a little while, as he'd driven to the pawnshop.

His parents' ranch house was located on the outskirts of town, not far from the Cherokee Cultural Center that had been such a big part of Rita's life.

The sprawling ranch had not only been where Clay had grown up, but also the place for many a town gathering. There was nothing his parents had enjoyed more than impromptu barbecues and parties with half the town of Cherokee Corners invited.

As he pulled up front and parked, he wondered if there would ever again be a party out here, if he would ever again see his mother act as gracious, fun-loving hostess for her neighbors and friends.

A light shone from the living room window and Clay assumed Sammy was probably watching a little late-night television. How nice, Clay thought, his anger once again knocking around inside him. Sammy was sitting on his father and mother's sofa, eating their food, watching their television, enjoying the comforts of their home after stealing and pawning jewelry that belonged to Clay's mom.

Long, determined strides carried Clay from his car to the front door. He wanted to hammer on the door, but knowing his father might be asleep, he held his control and knocked softly.

To his surprise it was his father who answered. "Clay…son." Thomas's features twisted into a mask of fear. "Is it…is there news?"

"No, no, Dad." Clay cursed himself. He should have known at this time of night his father would mistake his presence here for something official. "There's no news." The fear that had twisted his father's features left his face. "I just need to talk to Uncle Sammy…privately."

Thomas studied his son's face for a long moment, then turned and called over his shoulder. "Sammy, it's Clay and he wants to talk to you outside."

There was a long pause, then Sammy appeared in the doorway. "Clay. What's up?"

Samuel James was still a handsome man despite the fact that he was pushing sixty years old. He had a baby face, relatively unlined and thick black hair that Clay suspected he colored to keep away the gray.

His eyes were blue…guileless as a young boy's, but Clay wasn't fooled by the innocence radiating from those blue depths.

"Come on out here where we can talk," Clay said and stepped off the porch. He felt his blood boiling and reminded himself that punching his uncle might make him feel better, but would upset his father and wouldn't solve anything. Still, the thought of fist connecting with jaw was appealing.

"What's going on, Clay?" Sammy left the porch

and stood in front of Clay, his expression as innocent as a newborn babe. "Is something wrong?"

"I took a little drive to Shadow Hills tonight." Clay watched his uncle's face closely. A flash of something crossed Sammy's eyes. "Visited a place called Lucky's. Ever heard of it?"

Sammy sighed and swiped a hand through his hair as he took two steps backward from Clay. "Clay…I needed the money. I owed some people and they weren't willing to wait."

It enraged Clay that the first words out of Sammy's mouth wasn't an apology, but rather a rationalization for his crime. Unable to help himself, he stepped forward and punched Sammy with a finger in the chest. "What were you thinking? How could you have stolen from her? From Dad?"

"I was going to get them back! I pawned them, I didn't sell them. I was going to get the money to get them out of hock and figured nobody would be the wiser."

Clay's desire to hit him…hit something…anything… consumed him. His head ached with the chaos of the emotions that battled inside him. It was bad enough that Sammy had pawned anything of his mother's, but the fact that he'd pawned things she loved only made it worse.

Someplace in the back of his mind he knew he was angrier than the situation warranted. His subconscious mind knew that his rage wasn't just because Sammy had stolen his mother's jewelry, but was also because his father had been attacked, his mother had been taken away, and he couldn't get a handle on who was responsible.

"Clay." Thomas's voice came from the front door,

sounding as weary as it had since the day he'd come home from the hospital. "Go home, son. I'll take care of this."

Clay stood his ground, unwilling to let his father take care of it, unable to release the anger that still swelled inside of him. "He took her jewelry, Dad. The jewelry you'd bought for her. He took it and he pawned it."

"What difference does it make?" Thomas cried. "What damn difference does it make? She's gone. She's been gone for so long. We're never going to get her back...never." With a strangled sob, Thomas stumbled back into the house.

Thomas's utter hopelessness was like a mule kick to the gut for Clay. He reeled backward, watching as Sammy hurried after his father into the house.

We're never going to get her back...never. The words reverberated around and around in Clay's head With his stomach churning sickly both with anger and despair, he turned on his heel and headed back to his car. He peeled away from the house, spewing gravel from his back tires until he hit the highway.

He headed away from town, unwilling to do as his father had said and go home until some of the emotions inside him had quieted.

His father's loss of hope had been the final blow that had broken him. He'd been so strong through the entire ordeal, but he didn't feel strong now. Anger still tensed his shoulders and burned in his stomach. But the anger was mixed with other emotions too raw to identify.

He punched on his radio and tuned it to a favorite oldie station, hoping the sound of music would somehow soothe the beast inside him. But the light, rhythmic music only served to irritate him more.

He punched it off, opened his window to allow in the night air and fought off a press of emotion so intense he felt as if he might die.

Drawing deep breaths to steady himself, he knew that when the anger passed he'd be left with a painful, hollow emptiness.

He needed peace, but he didn't know how to get it. He needed a respite from his thoughts, from the brutal guilt and fear that assailed him more and more with each day that passed.

What if they never found his mother? Or worse, what if she was eventually found in a field, like Riley Frazier's mother had been…dead for months?

What if he never got an opportunity to see her snapping black eyes again, to see her beautiful smile, to tell her that he loved her? What if he couldn't bring her home to his father…a man who would never be the same without his beloved wife by his side?

The what-ifs could kill a man. They could slowly eat him from the inside out, like an insidious disease that can't be stopped.

Weariness tugged at him as well. The weariness of a man who had pushed himself too hard for too long. Since the night of his mother's disappearance, Clay's sleep had been plagued by nightmares.

In his tortured dreams his mother cried out to him, begging him to help her, begging him to find her. He ran, he hunted, he sought, but couldn't find her no matter how hard he tried.

He awakened each morning more exhausted than when he'd gone to sleep. If he could just have a few hours of dreamless sleep, if he could just have a moment in time where he felt at peace, then perhaps he could work more efficiently, find the clues that would lead to his mother.

He pulled his car to a halt and shut off his engine and headlights, shocked to find himself in front of Tamara's little cottage.

What was he doing here? What crazy impulse had led him to this particular place?

The house was dark. He glanced at his wristwatch. It was after midnight. Of course the place was dark. She was probably in bed, dreaming the dreams of the innocent.

He should go. He reached for the keys to start the engine once again, but before he could, the porch light blinked on and the front door opened.

Tamara stepped out on the porch. Clad in a yellow robe that matched the yellow scrap of silk Clay had seen flung on her bed, she looked like a vision from a dream.

As if in a dream he got out of his car and approached where she stood. He felt no anticipation or expectation. He just felt numb...completely and utterly void of any kind of emotion.

"I don't know...I don't know what I'm doing here," he began haltingly. "I just...I need..." he broke off, appalled by his own confusion.

"Come inside, Clay," she said softly. She opened the door to allow him entry.

He hesitated only a moment. He had no idea what forces had brought him here to her, had no idea what he needed from her, but as he entered the cozy cottage, he knew this was exactly where he needed to be at the moment.

* * *

Tamara hadn't been asleep when she'd heard his car. In fact, she'd been lying in bed thinking about him…worrying about him.

The tension that had filled the car on the way home from Lucky's Pawnshop had been nearly overwhelming. The anger that had simmered just beneath the surface in him had made her afraid, not for herself, but for him.

She'd recognized that he was a man on the verge of collapse, stressed by weeks of overworking, uncertainty and heartache.

She wondered about his confrontation with his uncle, but wouldn't ask what happened. She could tell by the dazed look in his eyes as he walked inside that he had reached his breaking point.

He stood in the center of the living room, as if unsure what to do next. He not only looked dazed and uncertain, he looked to be beyond exhaustion.

"Come on," she said softly and took him by the arm. "You need to sleep," she said to make sure he didn't misunderstand her actions.

She led him into her bedroom where a small lamp was lit on her nightstand. The window was open to allow in the sweet forest-scented night air and the tabletop fountain bubbled a soothing, rhythmic sound.

"Take off your shirt," she said. The dazed expression lifted from his eyes and he raised a dark brow. "Just your shirt, then lie down on your stomach on the bed." she added.

He asked no questions, but did as she requested. As he stretched out on her bed she reached into her nightstand drawer and removed a bottle of lavender oil.

She had no idea if what she was doing was right

or wrong, good or bad. She was moving on instinct and she rarely doubted her instincts.

"Just relax, Clay." She kneeled on the bed next to his prone body, careful not to make any physical contact. She didn't want him to get the wrong idea. "I'm just going to give you a little back rub to help relax you. This is going to be a bit cool."

He stiffened as she poured a liberal amount of the scented oil onto his broad back. She leaned over him and began to work the oil into his shoulder muscles with her fingertips.

His muscles were taut as bowstrings as she kneaded and smoothed over his bronze, warm skin. She tried to keep her mind carefully schooled away from the sensation of touching him and focused on the fact that she was trying to give him comfort in the only way she knew how.

But it was difficult not to notice that his attractive masculine scent filled the room, that his skin was soft and supple over the tight muscles. It was difficult not to notice the breathtaking expanse of his upper back that tapered into a slender waist.

It took several moments of her kneading and working his muscles before she felt them begin to relax. His breathing grew deeper…slower.

The only sound in the room was the rhythmic bubbling of the water fountain and Clay's deep, even breaths. She knew the instant he'd fallen asleep. The energy field that always emanated from him vanished and his muscles went lax beneath her hands.

Still she lingered, running her hands softly over his skin as a new kind of tension built inside her. Would she reject him if he turned over and took her in his arms? No, she had to admit to herself that she would not.

She scooted off the bed, careful not to awaken him. She stood by the edge of the bed for a long moment, taking the opportunity to gaze at him as he slept.

He nearly filled her double-size bed and she knew the scent of him would linger in the sheets until she decided to wash them again.

His mouth was slightly agape, making him look oddly vulnerable. She turned off the bedside lamp, deciding he wouldn't want her staring at him in the defenselessness of sleep.

She grabbed a blanket from a small utility closet, then went back into the living room and made a bed on the sofa. As she turned out the light, her thoughts were on the man sleeping in her bed.

She had no idea what had transpired from the time he'd dropped her off and the time that he'd returned. But it had been a near-broken man who had shown up on her doorstep.

Taking off her robe, she settled in on the sofa, the light blanket covering her. She had no idea what the morning would bring, what kind of a mood Clay would wear in the dawn of day.

His mood might have been better if she'd made an instantaneous decision that what he needed was to be held in her arms, made love to with a passion that stole away all other thoughts from his head.

However, she knew making love to Clay would be a foolish thing to do. She learned by her mistakes, and part of her life experience with Max had taught her that having a relationship with a man who didn't share your beliefs and core values only ended up in heartache.

Making love with Clay would be a mistake on her part, but she had a feeling it would be an enormous complication in his life. The last thing he needed was a personal relationship with anyone. He had more than enough emotional drama in his life with his missing mother and the serial killer.

She fell asleep with the memory of his skin beneath her fingers and the evocative scent of him invading her senses.

She awakened just before dawn, for a moment disoriented as she realized she'd slept on the sofa. Then she remembered. Clay.

Pulling on her robe, she went to the bedroom door, surprised to see Clay still asleep in her bed. She quietly pulled the door closed, then padded into the kitchen.

As she waited for the sun to come up and the coffee to brew, she wondered how long he would sleep. When she'd fallen asleep the night before she'd half expected him to be gone before she awakened. The fact that he was still asleep told her he'd been even more exhausted than she'd thought.

She poured herself a cup of coffee and sat at the table in the predawn light, unable to find thoughts in her head that didn't have to do with Clay.

She wondered if he'd always been as intense…as driven as he seemed. Certainly Rita had worried about his workaholic tendencies, but his mother had also considered Clay a lost soul, a man who had lost his spirituality and no longer listened to the beat of his Cherokee blood through his veins.

Tamara certainly didn't have the energy to heal a wounded man, nor did she want to fall in love with one. She was in the process of pouring herself a second cup of coffee when she sensed she wasn't alone.

She turned to see him standing in the kitchen doorway. Shirtless and barefoot, with his jeans riding low across his slender hips and his hair tousled from sleep, he momentarily stole her breath away.

"What time is it?" he asked. He looked sexy and handsome and cranky as a bear.

"Almost seven." She gestured toward the coffeepot. "Help yourself."

He frowned, irritation still riding his features. "Just a fast cup." He walked over to the cabinet and pulled down a mug as she resumed her seat at the table. "I can't believe I slept so long. What did you do? Work some sort of Cherokee hocus-pocus?"

"You know better than that," she said dryly. "I'd say you slept because you were exhausted."

He poured himself a cup of coffee, but remained standing by the counter instead of joining her at the table. He took a sip of the coffee, then looked at her, his gaze as obscure as she'd ever seen it.

"Thank you for your hospitality last night," he said. But his tone didn't hold any real gratitude, rather he sounded somewhat resentful. "I don't even know why I wound up here last night."

He took another sip of his coffee, then continued. "I guess I just needed to crash someplace peaceful and that's one thing I've noticed about this place…a sense of peace."

His voice still held a tinge of irritation. Apparently Clay James wasn't a morning person. He finished his coffee in a couple of swallows, then placed the mug in the sink. "I've got to get on my way."

He didn't wait for her reply, but instead strode out

of the kitchen. Tamara silently watched him go. She had a feeling his foul mood was more than just the possibility that he might not be a morning person.

She had a feeling his mood was because he was angry...embarrassed that she'd seen him weak, seen him vulnerable. She was certain he wasn't a man who showed weakness on a regular basis, if ever.

He returned to the kitchen moments later, dressed and obviously eager to be on his way. "Just wanted to say thanks again."

"It was no problem." She got up and walked with him to the front door. "You need to take care of yourself, Clay. I know you're under a lot of pressure with your work, but you can't work yourself to death."

He nodded, his gaze still dark and impenetrable. "You know, you're always welcome here if you need a place to unwind," she continued. "It is a peaceful place, that's why I love it."

His eyes seemed to grow darker, but with a spark of fire in their centers. "If I come here again and you welcome me inside wearing that yellow robe and nightie, it won't be sleep I'm looking for." His voice held both seduction and warning.

He didn't wait for her reply, but stepped out of the door and into the early morning sunshine. It was a good thing he hadn't waited for a reply from her. Her mouth had gone so dry she couldn't have formed a single word.

She watched as his car pulled away from the cottage, then closed and locked the door behind her. For a long moment she leaned against the door, fighting against the river of want that flowed through her.

Paint. That's what she needed to do. Painting would take her mind off the man she shouldn't have. Painting would still the haunting question of what it might be like to make love to a man like Clay.

Chapter 8

Appalled. Clay was appalled by his actions of the night before. What had he been thinking? To show up on Tamara's doorstep numb and depleted both physically and emotionally. He should have gone home or crawled into a hole until he was once again ready to face the world.

He'd still been able to smell the scent of the oil she'd used the night before when he'd awakened and he hadn't been able to wait to get home and shower it off. He'd needed not only to sluice off the flowery scent, but also the feel of her hands on his back.

Even now, after showering and leaving his own house, his back still seemed to retain the memory of her strong, yet soft fingers. He felt the whisper of silk against his side and remembered there had been a moment when he'd wanted nothing more than to turn over, take her into his arms and lose himself in making love to her.

Thank God he hadn't followed through on that particular weakness. It was bad enough that she'd seen him in the condition he'd been in when he'd arrived at her house. That would never happen again.

Sunday mornings the police station worked on skeleton crew, with only five officers on duty and nobody working in the lab. The good people of Cherokee Corners seemed to honor the Sabbath and kept their crimes spree to the weekdays.

It had been his intention when he left his house to go into the station, but instead he found himself heading toward Jacob Kincaid's place near the center of town.

If there was a grand mansion in the entire state of Oklahoma, it was Jacob's home. The unofficial history of the house was that an eccentric millionaire had built it for the young woman he intended to marry. The story went that the young lady traveled from New York to Cherokee Corners, took one look at the dusty small town and got on the next train back home.

The millionaire left the house half-finished and put in on the market for a song. Jacob's grandfather had bought it and finished the building.

The stately brick home set in the middle of a perfectly manicured three-acre lot. A long half-circle driveway led to the front of the house.

As he parked in the front, he checked his watch, noting that it was just before eight. Jacob should be home. He never worked on the weekends.

Considering the grandeur amid which Jacob lived, he was a surprisingly simple man with a taste for beautiful things. Clay wasn't surprised when Jacob greeted him at the door clad in a plaid bathrobe and slippers.

"Clay! Come in…come in. I've got a cup of coffee with your name on it."

"Thanks. I just thought I'd drop in for a quick cup and a short visit before heading into the station." Clay stepped into a foyer the size of his own living room. The gray marble floor beneath his feet shone with a luster and instantly reminded him of Tamara's eyes.

He followed Jacob quickly across the foyer and into the living room, which was actually a misnomer for what was actually Jacob's collection room.

Although the room had a sofa, love seat and coffee tables, the items of furniture were merely incidental to the true viewpoints in the room—the massive lighted display cases that lined every available wall.

Fabergé eggs, bronze statues, jeweled snuffboxes— Jacob liked flashy, beautiful things and the house was a testimony to that fact. Clay knew there was a room upstairs devoted entirely to priceless original oil paintings and another of antique furniture of museum quality.

Jacob led him into a huge, airy kitchen. This was the only room where there weren't items of interest or obsession. It was an ordinary kitchen and the one place in the house Clay had always felt at home.

The morning paper was stretched out on one side of the glass-top table along with a cup of coffee. Jacob gestured toward the table as he grabbed a cup from the cabinet and poured coffee for Clay then joined him at the table.

"You look better than you did when I stopped in the station. Did you finally get a good night's sleep?"

"Yeah, I did. I guess that the past few weeks finally caught up with me and I crashed hard." He didn't mention where he'd slept. There was no reason to talk about Tamara, no reason to even think about her. "We thought we had a lead to Mom last night."

"Really?" Jacob leaned forward, his gaze intent. "What happened?"

Briefly, Clay told him about the trip to Shadow Hills and the pawnshop. When he told Jacob about discovering that it had been Sammy who had pawned the jewelry, Jacob leaned back in his chair with the expression of one whom had eaten something sour.

"Doesn't surprise me a damn bit. Sammy never had a good sense of right and wrong," Jacob said gruffly. "The man has been nothing but heartache for your father. Your uncle Sammy makes me grateful I'm an only child."

"Lately I feel like an only child," Clay said dryly. "Since Bree got married and now with Savannah engaged to Riley, I feel like the odd man out."

"You aren't getting any younger, Clay. You should be married and with a family of your own."

"That's not in my plans." Clay took a sip of his coffee, then continued. "Being alone hasn't seemed to bother you." Clay eyed the older man curiously. "Why didn't you ever marry, Jacob?"

"Never found a perfect woman." He took a drink of his coffee, his eyes filled with reflection. "That was always a problem with me. I'd see a woman for a while but it didn't take me long to realize that what I believed was a perfect diamond was actually flawed. Too picky for my own good." He gestured toward the living room. "So, I've built a life collecting perfect pieces…flawless gems, surrounding myself with beauty instead of children."

"And you never regretted not having a family?"

"I'm a man at peace, Clay. I'm a man more comfortable alone. You, on the other hand, are far too young to make that kind of decision. From everything I've heard, there's nothing better for a man than the love of a good woman."

Clay finished his coffee, uncomfortable with the talk about good women and love. What he wanted to do was go by his parents' house and check on his father.

He wanted to make sure that the emotional turmoil of Sammy's betrayal hadn't destroyed his father more than he was already devastated by Clay's mom's absence.

"I think I'll head over to the house and check on Dad," Clay said as he rose from the table.

Jacob looked at him in surprise. "This was a fast visit."

"Sorry. I just feel like I need to stop by there, then I need to get to the lab. Sundays are quiet days and I can usually get a lot done."

Jacob stood as well and as they walked back through the living room, he clapped Clay on the back. "I'm sorry, son…about your uncle…about the hopes that I'm sure you felt as you drove to that pawnshop."

Clay shrugged with a nonchalance he didn't feel. "False leads and blind alleys are all part of the job."

"You'll keep me posted of any breaks in the case?" Jacob asked.

"Of course. Thanks for the coffee."

"Anytime."

As Clay left the house and walked down the flower-bordered walk to his car, he tried not to think of the woman who had opened her house to him in the middle of the night, a woman who hadn't questioned why he was there or what he might want. She'd simply opened her house and done what she'd thought was best for him.

A good woman. Perhaps Tamara was a good woman, but he wasn't in the market. He roared away from Jacob's house and headed toward the ranch, trying to keep his focus, his thoughts, his emotions in check.

He needed to check on his father, then get to work. Work would erase any crazy thoughts he might have about Tamara Greystone. Work would banish the memory of her wearing that little silk robe that he knew hid the tiny nightie beneath, would cast out the memory of her strong, yet gentle touch against his bare skin.

It took him only minutes to pull up in front of his parents' home. Savannah's car was out front. "Hey, brother," she greeted him as he walked into the living room.

Clay had always thought both his sisters were pretty, but each had blossomed with the new love in their lives. Savannah's eyes held a shine of happiness he hadn't seen in a long time and he knew it was Riley Frazier who had put the shine back into her eyes.

"Hey, sis. What are you doing here?"

"Dropped off a casserole. You know Uncle Sammy isn't much of a cook and Dad still isn't navigating the kitchen too well."

"Where are they?"

"They went to church." She swiped a strand of her long dark hair behind her ear. "Dad told me…about the jewelry."

Clay fought against the burst of anger that threatened to swell inside him. "Stupid ass didn't even use a fake identification."

She smiled wryly. "That's always been Uncle Sammy's problem. He's as inept at being a criminal as he is at being an upstanding citizen." Clay didn't return her smile. His blood still boiled as he thought of what Sammy had done.

"Well, I was just on my way out," Savannah said. "Riley is waiting for me at home."

Clay walked out on the front porch with her. "How long are you planning on commuting from Sycamore Ridge to here?" he asked. He knew the hour drive to and from work must be tiring for her.

Her dark eyes held his gaze. "Until Mom is returned to us. I don't want to leave the Cherokee Corners Police Department until we've got her back. Until then, I'll continue to drive in for work from Riley's place in Sycamore Ridge."

Clay nodded. He understood her desire to maintain status quo until they had all the answers where their mother's disappearance was concerned.

"Gotta run." She raised up on her tiptoes and gave him a quick kiss on the cheek.

He watched her get into her car and waved as she pulled away and for just a moment he felt as alone in the world as he'd ever felt.

He turned and walked back into the house. It no longer smelled like home. His mother's scent was absent and the very absence created an ache inside him.

As always when he was in the house, he eyed things critically, looking for things that might have been missed in the initial sweep right after the crime. Even though he knew the crime team had done a good job and he'd gotten in to pick up anything they might have missed, he never stopped looking.

He wandered the living room, then went down the hallway to his parents' bedroom. The bed was neatly made, probably thanks to Savannah, and the room looked just like it always had, but it felt different.

Instead of smelling like his mother's sweet perfume, the room smelled of his father's grief. He walked to his mother's side of the bed and stretched out on the blue floral spread.

He closed his eyes and tried to conjure up the sound of his mother's voice...not like he'd last heard it, when it had been filled with disappointment and aggravation, but rather her voice when she sang and laughed.

He'd taken for granted that he had many, many years with her. She was only fifty-five years old...still young but ready to welcome in the golden years of sharing love and life with her husband as well as her grown children.

It was the natural way of things that parents passed into the spirit world before their children, but not like this. Not stolen away and vanquished...not kidnapped and murdered...not found in a shallow grave in a field years later.

Again he was assailed with a wave of loneliness, mingling with the terror of the possibility that he would never see his mother alive again.

He sat up and shook his head, refusing to allow the terror to take hold. He had to believe that they'd find her alive. He had to believe that this was like Riley Frazier's mother's case.

Riley's mother had been missing for a year and a

half before she'd been murdered and eventually found in a field where Riley was building new homes.

Clay had to believe that same person who had taken Riley's mom had kidnapped his own mother, because that meant they might have time to find her before she was killed.

Time. He was wasting time here. He'd wasted time with Tamara. He should be working day and night, night and day to discover something—anything that would help find his mom.

He got up from the bed and was about to leave the room when a thread caught in the striker plate on the doorjamb captured his gaze. He leaned closer. Yes, it was a thread of some sort.

Under ordinary circumstances, Clay would have just assumed that his father had caught his pants or a shirt against the metal, but these weren't ordinary circumstances and Clay wasn't willing to take a chance that this single thread might not be important.

He had no bindles— the small paper envelopes that were used to collect evidence—with him. He went into the kitchen and withdrew a clean white envelope from one of the drawers, along with a spare pair of tweezers, then returned to the striker plate. Carefully, he removed the thread, placed it in the envelope, and then sealed it tight.

He checked his wristwatch, noting that it was just after ten. He had no idea how long his father and Sammy might be gone and decided he didn't want to wait around.

Carefully locking the door behind him, he left the house and got back into his car, the white envelope with the thread in it nearly burning a hole in his breast pocket. He wanted to get to the lab and check it out, although he knew better than to get his hopes up.

A single thread was little to go on. It was simply a tiny piece in an intricate puzzle. But if he got enough pieces and got very, very lucky, he might be able to put the puzzle together and find his mom.

Tamara painted all day Sunday, hoping to lose herself in the creative and lucrative work that she so loved. But the work didn't go well. She couldn't create the colors she sought, her perspective seemed off and she couldn't seem to immerse herself in the work enough to keep thoughts of Clay at bay.

By Monday afternoon she had to admit to herself that she was a bit disappointed that she'd heard no more from Clay. She knew it was ridiculous to have expected to hear from him, but somehow she had.

She told herself that he'd slept at her house, not with her, and owed her nothing. He'd thanked her Sunday morning when he left and he had nothing more to say to her.

Stifling a sigh, she checked her watch. There was still fifteen minutes of class time left. She'd given the students an assignment the moment they'd arrived. They were to pick a legend that they'd talked about in class and write a paper explaining both the legend and the student's emotional response to the legend. She intended to do the same thing with her adult class.

Maybe in reading the papers generated by the assignment she'd figure out who might be responsible for the vandalism in the classroom and the dead deer at her house.

She still figured it had all been a silly prank, but

that didn't mean the person responsible shouldn't have to face consequences.

There was only a week left of summer school and she was looking forward to the rest of summer without classes of any kind, when she could focus completely on her painting until the new school year started in September.

Max had called her the night before to see how she was progressing on the new paintings for the showing in Oklahoma City in the fall. They'd chatted a bit, then had hung up.

Tamara had been grateful that they'd been able to part ways personally, yet still maintain a good working relationship with each other. She'd been able to put her bitterness and hurt behind her where he was concerned. Max wasn't the man of her heart, but he was definitely the agent she wanted representing her in the art world.

"Okay, people," she said as she checked her watch once again. "Time's up. Please leave your papers on my desk and I'll see you all tomorrow."

She smiled at each of the students as they dropped their papers on her desk, then headed out the door. She was sure all of them would be just as happy as she was to see summer school come to an end.

She gathered up the papers as the last student disappeared out the doorway, then grabbed her purse and headed out of the building.

It had to be one of the hottest days of the year, she thought as she walked across the parking lot asphalt. Although she usually went directly to her cottage after summer school classes, she decided to drive to the Redbud Inn and read the papers while she indulged in a hot fudge sundae.

The ice cream parlor was jumping, with kids coming and going with ice-cream cones or sodas. Tamara waved to Alyssa who was working behind the counter, then took a seat at one of the small round tables in the corner.

She placed the papers on the table, then went up to the counter and stood in line behind a mother with two children who couldn't make up their minds what kind of ice cream they wanted.

As she patiently waited, she couldn't help but notice the dark shadows beneath Alyssa's eyes, shadows that told Tamara that her friend's visions probably hadn't retreated, but rather were attacking her as viciously as ever.

Her attention turned to the mother and two children and their conversation about ice cream.

"I want pretty ice cream, either blue like the sky or green like the grass," the little girl said. She was a dainty little thing, all ruffles and bows, about five years old.

"That's dumb," the boy exclaimed. He was obviously the older brother by a year or two. "It doesn't matter what it looks like. It matters what it tastes like."

"Let's just make up our minds," the mother said and flashed a glance of apology to Tamara. "There are other people waiting to get ice cream."

It took another minute or two for the two to decide, peanut butter fudge for the boy and strawberry marshmallow for the little girl who proclaimed that the light pink concoction looked just like a ballerina's tutu.

As the three left the shop, Tamara watched them, a wistful want fluttering through her. She wanted children. At thirty years old it wasn't just her biological

clock that was loudly ticking but it was a psychological clock as well. She'd wanted to have her children
by the time she reached this age, had wanted to grow
with them.

"Earth to Tamara."

She snapped her attention to Alyssa. "Sorry." Instantly her worry for her friend was back. "Are you
okay?"

Alyssa nodded. "Overworked as usual, but I'm
okay. Everything all right with you?"

"Fine, just thought I'd sit here in the cool and read
some papers while eating one of your famous hot
fudge sundaes."

"Sounds like a plan. One hot fudge sundae coming
right up."

A moment later Tamara was seated at her corner
table indulging her sweet tooth as she read papers.
When she came to one written on the legend of the
bear she set it on a separate stack to read later at
length.

When she finished the separation process, she had
five students who had chosen to write about the legend of the bear.

She was reading the second paper from that stack
when there was a lull in customers and Alyssa joined
her at the table.

"Want a cup of coffee or an iced tea or something?" she asked.

"No, I'm fine," Tamara assured her. For a few
minutes the two women talked of inconsequential
things, the warm weather, the new movie that was
showing at the only theater in town and plans for the
fall festival at the cultural center.

They spoke of their hopes that Rita would be back

home and able to take part in the ceremonies that had been so dear to her heart. An attractive young blond woman who approached their table interrupted their conversation.

"Alyssa, I'm sorry to bother you, but I was wondering if you could include a little more fruit on the breakfast menu. As you've probably noticed I never eat the eggs or bacon, but I do nibble on the whole wheat toast and I like my fruit in the mornings."

"I'll see what I can do, Virginia," Alyssa replied.

Tamara had recognized the woman's delicate features, but hadn't been able to place her until Alyssa said her name. Virginia. Virginia Maxwell, the wife of Greg Maxwell who'd been the first victim of the serial slasher.

As Virginia left, Alyssa cast a pained expression at Tamara. "I feel so sorry for her and I know she's going through a rough time, but she's driving me a little bit crazy with her demands."

"She's been staying here?" Tamara asked.

Alyssa nodded. "Ever since Greg's murder. She says she just can't face going home to her silent house yet."

"It's been a while since Greg's murder. In fact, it's been several weeks since Sam McClane was found dead. Maybe this serial slasher has left town. Maybe there won't be any more murders."

Alyssa's eyes were dark…haunted as she held Tamara's gaze. "It's not over. The killings aren't over at all. They've only just begun. I know it. I feel it here." She touched her heart. "And I see it inside here." She pointed to her head. "But let's not talk about it anymore, okay?"

It was obvious the conversation was upsetting her.

"Okay," Tamara agreed. They filled the next few minutes with more inane chatter, then a group of kids came in and Alyssa returned to the counter to wait on them.

Tamara tried to refocus on the papers, but her concentration had been broken and the noise level in the parlor had increased to a decibel that she knew would make further concentration difficult.

She gathered her papers, deciding to head home. She waved to Alyssa, then stepped back into the stifling late afternoon heat.

Despite the heat, a chill wiggled up her spine as she headed for her car. She knew the chill was due to Alyssa's words...that the killing wasn't over. And it didn't take long for her thoughts to segue from the crimes to the man who was attempting to solve them.

Clay. His scent had become trapped in her sheets the night he'd slept in her bed. Last night Tamara had slept with that bold, masculine scent enveloping her and she wished it had been his big, strong arms around her instead of just his scent.

She shook her head ruefully. There was definitely a touch of perversity in her soul...to want a man who had nothing to do with her dreams for her future. It was absolutely contrary of her to want to have anything to do with Clay James. And yet, perverse or not, contrary or not, she couldn't help the way even mere thoughts of him caused her heart to beat just a little bit faster.

She turned down the dirt lane to her cottage, trying to empty her mind of all thoughts. The first thing she intended to do when she got home was wash those sheets. Maybe if she could banish the scent of Clay from her cottage, she could banish thoughts of him from her mind.

As her cottage came into view, her heart slammed like a fist against her rib cage. The windows were shattered, the broken glass sparkling in the late afternoon sunshine. The front door stood agape sporting a fresh wound in the shape of the familiar claw mark. Blood shone like a garish grin.

For a long moment her mind refused to wrap around it all. She remained, engine idling in the place she had stopped, staring at the destruction before her.

Just as quickly as it had descended on her, the stunned inertia snapped. She backed down the lane as if the very devil himself was after her.

It wasn't until she pulled up in front of the police station that tears began to fall. Her home, a place of peace and serenity, had been violated.

Who was responsible? And how far were they willing to go to live the legend of the bear?

For the first time since her classroom had been vandalized, a sense of imminent danger swept through her. She got out of her car and hurried into the police station.

Chapter 9

Clay gazed around the living room. Even though he and his team had been inside for the past three hours collecting evidence, it was still a shock to see the utter destruction that had taken place.

The entire cottage smelled like unbridled rage. There appeared to be no method or control to the damage that had been wrought. It was as if a monster had gone berserk inside the walls of the place.

A monster. He remembered the vision Alyssa had told him about, a vision of Tamara being chased by a monster...killed by a monster.

He moved to the front window, which was now simply a glassless hole and saw Tamara leaning against a patrol car flanked by two officers.

She hadn't been inside yet. Nobody had been inside except Clay and his two-man forensic team. They had collected hairs and fibers, fingerprints and anything else that might have DNA or evidence potential.

He knew the officers had questioned her and she'd told them that she'd gone from summer school to the ice cream parlor.

It had been sheer luck that she'd chosen this day not to go directly home from summer school. The blood on the front door had still been tacky when Clay had arrived, indicating to him that Tamara had either just missed the perpetrator when she'd arrived here or the perp might have still been in the house when she'd pulled up.

Had she come directly home from school who knew what kind of scene Clay would now be processing? The very thought made his blood chill.

He turned from the window as Trey Morgan, who had been gathering evidence from the bedroom, entered the living room. "I think I got everything worth getting from the bedroom and bathroom," he said.

"You want to check and see if Burt needs help outside. I'm pretty much finished here, too."

Trey nodded and disappeared out the front door. Clay moved back to the front window and once again peered out at Tamara.

She was too far away for him to tell what kind of an expression rode her pretty features. He could easily imagine what her expression was going to be when she walked through the front door and viewed the shambles that had been her home.

It would have been easy for him to pack up his collected evidence and get to the lab, leaving it to the uniformed officers to bring her inside.

But he didn't intend to do that. He knew what had been destroyed here, and it was far more than mere furniture, knickknacks and personal belongings.

The aura of tranquility that he had noticed both

times he'd been inside the house was gone, shattered beneath the violence that had taken place here. And he wasn't sure that any amount of glue and cleanup would be able to restore that special air of serenity to the cottage.

When Trey came back inside, Clay gestured to the metal suitcase that carried all the samples he'd taken. "Would you mind dropping that off at the lab when you take your samples in? I'm going to hang out here and find out what Ms. Greystone intends to do. It's obvious she can't stay here for the night."

"Sure. If there's nothing more for us to do here, Randy and I will go ahead and take off."

"We're finished," Clay replied. "Store the samples and I'll start on them tomorrow."

The two men said goodbye and Trey left. There would be plenty of items for Clay to process the next day, but no certainty that anything they collected would lead to the perpetrator. Clay wondered how many of his own hairs Trey had collected off Tamara's bed.

He walked to the front door and as he exited the house, Tamara stood up and took a few steps toward him. They had not spoken at all since he'd arrived to begin his investigation.

As he drew closer to her, he saw that her gray eyes were somber, but there wasn't a trace of tears in their depths. Someplace deep inside him marveled at her strength.

"It's bad, isn't it," she said.

"It's bad," he confirmed. He looked at the two officers who stood nearby. "Somebody is going to have to keep on eye on the place until it's secured."

Jason, one of the two officers, nodded. "I've already given Jeb a call and told him we've got some work for him. He can board up the windows and secure the house until Ms. Greystone gets things back in order.''

''Good.'' Although Clay didn't like Jason Sheller, the man had always done his job efficiently. ''If Jeb is on his way, then Tamara and I can wait here for him and you two can get on back to the station house.''

Clay didn't speak to Tamara again until the two officers had gotten into their patrol car and started down the lane away from the house, only then did he direct his attention back to her.

''You know you can't stay here. The exterior damage is nothing compared to the interior damage. Is there someplace you can go for a couple of nights until you can get the mess cleaned up? What about your parents' place?''

She shook her head. ''My parents moved last year to a beautiful condo in Santa Fe and I know Alyssa has a full house right now. Don't worry, I'll think of something. Can I go inside now?''

Clay nodded, fighting the impulse to take her elbow, hold her hand, and somehow offer support as she walked through the place she had called home.

At that moment Jeb pulled up in his pickup. He'd come prepared with sheets of plywood and the tools he would need to board up the broken windows.

If Cherokee Corners had an official handyman, it was Jeb Tanner. Skilled not only in carpentry, but also in plumbing and wiring as well, Jeb's truck was a familiar sight around town.

Clay didn't have to tell him what had to be done, the quiet young man simply went to work, pulling plywood from the back of the truck as he nodded to Clay.

Clay turned back to Tamara. "Ready?"

She nodded and they walked side-by-side up the porch stairs and to the front door. He heard the deep breath she drew before she stepped through the threshold and into what had been her living room.

"Oh." The single expression fell from her lips as she viewed the damage. She wrapped her arms around her stomach as if the sight made her stomach ache.

He followed her gaze around the room and felt as if he were seeing it all for the first time. Stuffing hung from the sofa, spilling from knife wounds that had rent the fabric. The beautiful collection of glass and crystal hummingbirds now crunched underfoot. Plants had been overturned, books ripped apart and the walls all had the mark of the bear claws scarring them.

He followed her into the kitchen, where the same kind of damage had been done. Cabinets had been ripped open, the contents crashed to the floor. Ceramic shards were all that was left of her dishes and mugs.

Again he found himself admiring the inner strength that seemed to hold her together. Her back remained ramrod straight, her eyes utterly tearless as she silently viewed all the things that had been broken.

For some reason, her unemotional calm bothered him more than if she'd screamed and cried with each discovery of ruin. It was as if her pain was too great for tears.

As they returned to the living room, he finally broke the silence. "You should gather some things together...clothes and toiletries...whatever you'll need until this place can be cleaned up and made livable again.''

''I can't believe this,'' she said. ''This took so much unbridled energy to do all this damage.'' When she looked at him her eyes were dark, like tumultuous storm clouds. ''This frightens me.''

''It should,'' he said more gruffly than he intended. Again he felt the need to pull her against him, chase away that darkness in her eyes…darkness he knew was the result of fear.

He certainly was no stranger to fear. He woke up with it every morning, went to bed with it as his nightly companion. The fear for his mother was a constant ache in his chest and he knew she must be feeling that same kind of uncertainty.

She picked up a torn canvas with a half-finished painting from the floor. ''Nothing was spared, was it?''

Clay jammed his hands in his jeans pockets as if to stop himself from reaching out to her. ''It would appear not.''

''I'll just go get some things together.'' She started for the bedroom, but had taken only a step or two when she cried out and bent to the floor.

He couldn't see what it was that had caused her pain, but when she stood she held two pieces of something wooden in her hands and as she looked at him her eyes filled with tears. ''It was my mother and father's courting flute.'' She bit her bottom lip as tears trailed down her cheeks. ''How could anyone be so cruel?''

Clay pulled his hands from his pockets and gently took the two pieces of wood from her. Someplace in the back of his mind he knew that taking the wood was far safer than taking her into his arms. "Go get your things," he said gently.

She swiped at her tears and disappeared into the bedroom. He didn't follow her. Instead he remained in the living room and stared down at the two pieces of wood in his hand.

He could hear the sounds of Jeb's hammering coming from someplace in the back of the house. He assumed he was covering the bedroom windows that had been broken.

His fingers rubbed against the smooth wood of the broken flute. He remembered his mother telling him about the courting flute, that when a Cherokee man fell in love, he went to the river and searched for the perfect river cane to make into a flute. He then supposedly listened to his heart and composed a song for his loved one.

Clay knew nothing about composing songs, but he did know how important it was to follow his gut instinct, and his gut instinct was singing to him that Tamara was in danger.

She came out of her bedroom carrying a suitcase. Her shoulders now slumped and her eyes appeared reddened, indicating to him she'd shed a few more tears while packing her things.

"Tamara, it's clear to me that you are in danger," he said, deciding not to mince words. "If this is, indeed, an enactment of the legend of the bear, we both know the ending isn't exactly happy for the young Native maiden."

"I don't know what to do.... I don't even know where to go."

"You can come to my place," Clay said, making the decision instantly. "I've got plenty of room and you'll be safe there. In fact we'll leave your car here, so nobody will see it around my house and know where you are.''

''You really think that's necessary?'' Her eyes were huge, filled with more vulnerability than he'd ever seen.

''I think you need to give us a couple of days to see if we can round up who is responsible for this. In the meantime it would be good if you kept an invisible profile and the best place to do that is at my house.'' He flashed her a dry smile. ''Nobody ever comes to visit me.''

Tamara felt as if she had been thrust onto the back of a wildly galloping horse. It seemed as if one minute she'd been standing in the ruins of her own home and the next minute she was being led down the hallway of Clay's ranch house to a spare bedroom.

She felt as if her brain had been wrapped in cloth and wasn't quite firing on all cylinders. The only emotion she seemed able to sustain at the moment was sheer, bone-aching exhaustion.

She scarcely looked around the room as Clay left her alone. All she wanted was to go to bed and wake up in the morning and realize this had all been nothing more than a bad dream.

It took her only minutes to take off her clothes and pull on her nightgown, then she slid beneath the crisp white sheets of the double bed and stared up at the dark ceiling.

It frightened her, the destruction that had been done to her home. And what frightened her more was the thought that if she hadn't gone to the ice cream parlor she would have been in the cottage.

What would have happened to her had she been home? And who was responsible? Who had done such a terrible thing? It was difficult for her to believe that one of her students was responsible. This wasn't some sort of bad prank or joke. It was something more evil than that, something more dangerous than that.

It took a while for her to fall asleep. Her surroundings were unfamiliar both in scent and in sound. The central air was hushed compared to her window unit at the cottage, although definitely more efficient. The room was void of scent, as if nobody had ever stayed here before.

She finally fell asleep and dreamed of bears. The big creatures were everywhere, hiding in her closets, slinking behind trees, watching her...waiting for her...wanting her.

When she woke up she knew instantly that it was far later than she normally slept. The sun was already high in the sky as she sat up and looked around the room where she'd spent her restless night.

The room was just as she'd remembered from the night before, clean and austere with just a bed and a chest of drawers for furniture.

She got out of bed and pulled on the short yellow robe that matched her nightie, then remembering what Clay had said about that particular attire, she grabbed a pair of jeans and a T-shirt from her suitcase and changed into them before leaving the bedroom.

She didn't hear a sound as she followed the hallway into the living room. Living room was what the room was supposed to be, but it was more laboratory than anything. Two upholstered chairs and a television were the only items to attest that the room was perhaps occasionally used for living and relaxing, not just working.

However the rest of the room was testimony to Clay's work obsession. A stainless steel worktable stood along one wall, holding a complicated-looking microscope and high-powered lamps. There were several other pieces of equipment as well, but she steered clear from all of them.

Instead she breathed a sigh of relief as she stepped into a large, airy, quite ordinary kitchen. The scent of coffee lingered in the air, but the pot on the countertop was empty. In front of the coffeepot was a note from Clay telling her to make herself at home and not to go anywhere.

Where was she going to go? She had no car. At the moment she had no home, at least not one that was livable. As she waited for a pot of coffee to brew she studied the note that Clay had written.

His handwriting was bold...strong, a reflection of the man himself. She pushed the note aside and rubbed the center of her forehead as she thought of her cottage. An edge of anger rose up inside her. She hated the fact that some creep had chased her away from her home.

Last night she'd been filled with fear. This morning she had more anger inside her than fear. She got up and poured herself a cup of coffee, then stood at the kitchen window and stared outside.

Clay's house was just inside the city limits on the west side of Cherokee Corners. His only neighbor appeared to be an old oil drill that stood unmoving like a frozen, mechanical giant insect.

Funny that he had chosen a place as isolated as she had to live. Her art and the need to regroup after leaving Max had drawn her to the cottage in the woods. She wondered what had driven Clay to this empty stretch of road and the house in the middle of farmer fields?

She returned to the table and drank two cups of coffee before heading back down the hallway to the bathroom for a shower. After showering and dressing once again, she stood in the doorway of the bathroom and gazed down the hall. She knew the first bedroom on the left was where she'd slept the night before.

The other two bedroom doors were open and she walked down the hall and peered into the first one. It was obviously used as a home office. Bookshelves lined the walls and a desk held a massive computer system.

The other bedroom was Clay's and it was the one room in the house that held any signs of real life. The bed was unmade, the sheets twisted as if to indicate the person who'd slept here had not enjoyed a restful night.

The dresser top was littered with odds and ends, loose change, brown paper envelopes, several bottles of cologne and a childish drawing of a forest filled with elflike little people and signed to Uncle Clay with love from Maggie.

The room held his scent, that clean masculine smell that had enchanted her from the first moment she'd met him. She backed out of the room, reminding herself that she wasn't here because Clay wanted her here, or because she wanted to be here. She was in his home for her own safety. He'd just been doing his job in inviting her into his personal space.

She was seated in one of the two chairs in the living room, sketching on a pad she'd salvaged from her bedroom closet the night before when Clay returned home at noon.

"Hope you like burgers and seasoned fries," he said as he came in carrying a sack from a drive-through. "Even if it isn't your favorite, it's better than what you'll find in my refrigerator."

"Burgers and fries are fine," she said. She put her sketch pad down and followed him into the kitchen. He pointed her to a chair as he distributed the food onto paper plates. "I'll pick up some groceries this afternoon. I'm not used to having a houseguest. Iced tea?"

She nodded and sat at the table. He seemed wired up, filled with reckless energy and she didn't say anything to him until he was seated next to her. "Busy morning?" she asked.

"Yeah, instead of working in the lab, I've been interviewing some of your students, checking out their whereabouts yesterday after school."

"Which ones?"

"According to his mother, Terry Black came right home from school yesterday to help clean out their garage. You were right, the kid has a bad temper. He wasn't happy about me asking questions about him, got into my face a bit, but I set him straight."

She didn't ask how. She only knew that if the burly teenager and Clay went head to toe, her money would be square on the man seated across the table from her.

"So, he has an alibi for yesterday afternoon," she said.

Clay shrugged. "A mother's alibi...not exactly without suspicion. On the other hand, Charlie Tamer has an airtight alibi. He was at a counseling session with his psychologist. I checked it out with his doctor and he was there all right.''

"What about my class this afternoon? And the adult class tonight?''

"I spoke with Will Nichols this morning and he agreed that you're finished teaching for the summer. He said with just a week left it was ridiculous to take chances with your safety. I agreed with him.''

She frowned thoughtfully and toyed with one of her fries. "Don't you think maybe we're overreacting a bit?''

His gaze held hers with a light of disbelief. "Have you forgotten what happened at your cottage yesterday? Have you forgotten that in your legend the bear wreaks havoc to show his prowess before he corners the Native maiden and kills her? Are you willing to take a chance that whomever is responsible for this is going to stop before he reaches the end of the legend?''

"No.'' The word fell from her lips in a grudging whisper.

"Look, I know you don't particularly want to be here, but you need to be someplace safe until we figure out who is behind all this. The bad news is, I'm not a great host. The good news is I'm not home much.''

His words should have assured her, but they didn't. "I just feel like I'm imposing.'' In truth, even though she had only spent a single night and half a day here, she already felt ill at ease.

But it wasn't because he might be a poor host, it was because having seen the bed where he slept, she wanted to sleep there, too. It was because her desire for Clay James was reaching a proportion that was getting more and more difficult to ignore.

He watched her on the cameras that were built into the ceiling of her rooms and gave him a bird's-eye view of everything she did.

She had yet to open the dress box he'd sent in through the slot in her locked door. She'd carried it to the bed and now stood staring at it as if afraid of what it might contain.

She need not have been afraid. The dress box contained exactly what it was meant to hold...a lovely gown. He'd ordered it specifically for her, knowing the coral color would look exquisite next to her bronze skin.

A sweet rush of anticipation swept through him as he watched her. He could already imagine her in the gown. She would look so beautiful.

He was rushing things a bit with her. With the others he'd waited three months before making his first contact and giving them a gown. But with Rita, he was as anxious as a schoolboy, eager to know that finally, finally he'd gotten the one that was meant to last forever.

As she sat on the edge of the bed and drew the box closer to her, he felt a bead of sweat run down the side of his face. "Open it, my sweet," he said to himself. He could have flipped an intercom button and spoken directly to her, but he knew it was far too soon for that kind of personal contact.

"Open it and put it on. Wear it for me." His hands clenched into sweaty fists as he continued to watch the screens.

She picked up the box and shook it, then once

again set it on the bed and drew off the lid. He watched closely as she pulled away the white tissue paper to expose the coral silk.

She withdrew the gown from the box and held it up. His breath caught painfully in his chest. It was like a coral waterfall, so beautiful. The only thing that would make it better was if it was on her, draping from her proud breasts, emphasizing her slender waist.

"Put it on." His heartbeat raced faster than he could remember as he willed her to do as he bid.

There was no way to anticipate her actions, no way to be prepared for what she did. She appeared completely calm as she held the dress in front of her, then with a cry of sudden outrage, she began to rip the dress apart in a frenzy.

He heard the tearing of the expensive material, along with her screams of outrage. His heartbeat slowed and the sweet anticipation he'd felt only moments before faded.

Too soon. She wasn't yet ready to accept his gifts. He shut off the cameras and leaned back in his chair, fighting a wave of disappointment. Oh well, he'd been disappointed before. Patience. He needed to have a little patience.

He'd been patient before. Unfortunately in the other two cases, his patience hadn't been rewarded.

He hoped Rita was different. He hoped he didn't have to start the process all over again for the fourth time.

Chapter 10

Clay had thought it wouldn't be difficult having her in his house, but he'd been wrong. He'd thought because she seemed even-tempered, undemanding and generally pleasant that he'd hardly notice her presence. He'd definitely been wrong.

For the past three days that she'd been in his house, he'd been on a slow burn. Her scent eddied in the air, filling his nose and seeping into his pores. She'd brought a new energy to the house that he found both irritating and pleasing.

For the past two nights he'd been kept awake by visions of her in that damnable nightgown, visions that kept him tossing and turning with the desire to make love to her.

She'd even brought in several handfuls of wildflowers and placed them in glasses around the kitchen, adding color and scent to what had otherwise been austere surroundings.

He now eyed her across the kitchen table, wondering if she could feel his desire for her. How could she not be aware of it? It seemed to be taking complete possession of him.

She'd surprised him by having dinner ready when he'd come in from the lab at seven. It was a fairly simple meal of meat loaf, mashed potatoes and corn, but it was the best meat loaf, the creamiest mashed potatoes and the sweetest corn he'd ever eaten.

"You're a good cook," he said, breaking the silence that had grown to mammoth proportions between them since he'd come home.

She shrugged, her shoulders bare and looking far too touchable beneath the light pink sundress she wore. "I like to cook when I have somebody to cook for besides myself."

"Why aren't you married?" He could tell the question took her by surprise. In truth, it surprised him. But now that he had asked it he was genuinely curious. "You're an attractive woman, a good cook, talented and bright. Why are you all alone?"

She dabbed at her mouth with her napkin before replying. "Haven't found the right man." She hesitated a moment, then continued, "I thought I did once, but he turned out to be Mr. Wrong."

"Somebody from around here?"

She shook her head, her hair moving like a curtain of shine around her head. "No, somebody from New York. My agent, actually. His name is Max Bishop. He's a wonderful agent, but he wasn't the right partner for me."

"Why not?"

She flashed him an impish smile that stirred a flame deep in the pit of his stomach. "I just want to warn you, when I finish answering your questions, I intend to ask you a few of my own.''

He started to protest, then slowly nodded. "Fair enough. Now tell me about this Max Bishop.''

She pushed her plate to the side and leaned back in her chair, her gray eyes taking on the look of reflection. "I met Max at an art show in Oklahoma City. He was touring the country looking for new blood. We got to talking, I showed him my work and he talked me into coming to New York and allowing him to be my agent. For the first couple of months that I was in New York our relationship was strictly business.''

"But that changed." He was surprised to feel just the tiniest flicker of jealousy as he thought of her being intimate with another man. It was a totally irrational piece of emotion that irritated him.

"Yes, that changed. Max seemed bigger than life to me. He was so enthusiastic about my work and I guess that made me enthusiastic about him. Anyway, our relationship became personal and I thought I'd found Mr. Right.''

"So, what happened?" Clay shoved his plate aside, no longer hungry for anything but information.

"What happened was that Max loved having a Native American artist to represent. He loved having me dress up in tear dresses and braids for art shows. He loved me talking about Cherokee legends and traditions as long as there was a buyer nearby who might be charmed by the pretty Indian squaw.''

Clay winced at the derogatory term. She got up from the table and carried her plate to the sink. She rinsed it and put it in the dishwasher then turned to face him once again, her eyes darkened by memories.

"The problem got even bigger. You see, Max wanted me to be Native when it suited his purpose, but he wanted me not to be Native when it was just the two of us. I tried to please him, but in doing so I realized I was slowly sacrificing my own self-identity."

"So you came back here to Cherokee Corners."

"And my Cherokee roots." She walked back to the table and took his plate, then carried it to the sink, rinsed it and put it in the dishwasher next to hers. "The man I intend to marry will be a man who is proud of where he comes from, a man who is steeped in the same traditions as me."

She sank back down at the table, her eyes shining with determination. "The man I marry will be a man like my father...a warrior who is proud of where he came from, a man sensitive enough to carve a court-ing flute for the woman he loves, a man strong enough to raise his family with the teachings of his traditions."

"Are you sure such a man exists?" Clay's voice held a touch of amusement.

She raised her chin slightly, as if to deflect any mockery he might point in her direction. "If he doesn't, then I'll remain alone. I won't settle for less than what I desire."

Her passion stirred him, even though he thought her a fool for having standards no real man would ever be able to meet. A proud warrior, indeed. He started to get up from the table but she surprised him by rising up and punching a finger in his chest to reseat him once again.

"You aren't finished yet," she said. "You've in-terrogated me, now it's my turn to interrogate you."

He smiled at her lazily, oddly enough enjoying the fact that she demanded turnabout fair play. "All right. What do you want to know?"

"Why aren't you married? You're an attractive man, pleasant enough when you want to be."

"I haven't found too many people worth being pleasant to," he countered. "Besides, as I indicated to you before, I have no desire to marry. I like my life just as it is."

"All work and no play," she scoffed. "Even your living room is more lab than living room."

"Crime-scene investigator is who I am."

"No it isn't, it's what you do," she countered.

He grinned. "A mere matter of semantics. I like my work."

"But what about relationships? Don't you miss having companionship…" Her voice trailed off and she looked down at the table as her cheeks turned a dusty rose.

His grin widened. "Are you asking me about sex, Tamara? I can tell you that I like sex…a lot. That's the only kind of relationship I'm interested in, strictly physical without the complications of emotions or commitment."

She directed her gaze back to him again, her cheeks still holding a tinge of pink color. "Why don't you have anything to do with the cultural center? Your entire family participates there. Why don't you?"

He stood suddenly. "I think I've answered enough questions for one night. Thanks for the good meal. I've got some work I want to do in the living room."

He was grateful she didn't try to stop him as he left the kitchen. He didn't want to talk about the cultural center. He didn't want to talk about his Native roots. As far as he was concerned, being Cherokee wasn't a blessing, it was a curse.

Tamara wanted a proud warrior and he was neither proud nor a warrior. All he wanted to do was solve crimes and he had more on his plate at the moment in that respect than he knew what to do with.

He was no closer to finding his mother. Even though the Oklahoma City lab had returned some of the results of forensic testing from the two serial killer cases, there was nothing that pointed a finger to a particular culprit. And now he needed to find out who was terrorizing Tamara so he could get her out of his house and back in her own before something happened between them that would only lead to regret.

It took Tamara only minutes to finish cleaning up the kitchen. As she worked, her mind went over the conversation she'd just shared with Clay.

He'd simply confirmed what she'd already known, that despite the fact that he made her pulse race just a little too fast, in spite of the fact that she was growing more and more hungry for his kiss, for his touch, he was definitely not the man for her.

He liked sex a lot. His words evoked a river of heat to rush through her. He liked it and she imagined he was quite good at it.

She left the kitchen and went into the living room where Clay sat on a stool at the worktable peering into the microscope. She sat in one of the upholstered chairs and picked up her sketch pad. She'd love to sketch him, but she had a feeling he wouldn't be pleased so she contented herself by working on a picture that would be her next painting.

Besides, she needed something to keep her focus

off Clay, because looking at him evoked yearnings she was better off ignoring.

Instead of a bear, the picture she worked on was of a wolf. She'd never tried painting one before and found the work both challenging and fulfilling.

She had never told anyone about her relationship with Max before and she'd found that telling Clay had been cathartic. It had pleased her to realize that those days and nights with Max seemed like a different lifetime ago, that there was no pain or heartache resulting from that particular mistake.

"You can turn on the television if you want," Clay said.

"No, I don't mind the silence." She hesitated a moment, then added. "You have a lot of equipment here."

"The lab down at the station is so small and most of this I bought with my own money." He straightened up and took the slide he'd been looking at out of the microscope. "I can't do anything official here...chain of evidence and all that nonsense. But I do a lot of unofficial work here. Retesting, reevaluating and looking at things that we've determined probably have no evidentiary value."

"Why would you look at things you've already dismissed as useless?" she asked. It wasn't so much that she had a burning need to know, but rather because he seemed to be in a talkative mood, unlike the past two evenings they had shared together.

The past two nights had been both silent and tense. She'd retreated to her bedroom early on both nights.

He flashed her a quick grin. "Because sometimes we make mistakes."

"How are all your investigations going?"

His smile fell. "Slow. I got some reports back this morning from a lab in Oklahoma City pertaining to Greg Maxwell's and Sam McClane's murders, but whoever committed the murders was smart and left precious little physical evidence behind."

"I heard that at one time Virginia Maxwell was a potential suspect."

"That was before Sam's murder. Whenever somebody is killed, the spouse is usually the first person to be checked out. But nobody could find any reason why Virginia would want her husband dead, and there was definitely no connection between her and Sam."

She set her sketch pad down. "It's hard for me to believe a woman could be capable of those murders. But of course, it's hard for me to believe that anyone could be capable of such a thing."

"Our work is becoming more and more difficult as more television shows show the procedures we use to gather physical evidence," he said. "We're raising a bunch of savvy criminals who know way too much about transfer and forensic science."

"So, you haven't been able to find anything to help in solving the crimes?"

"We've got a few things, but I'm really not at liberty to discuss them."

"I understand," she replied. She hesitated a moment before speaking again. "Have you found anything worthwhile in the evidence you collected at the cottage?" He hadn't mentioned much of that particular investigation.

"Afraid not. So far all we've really gotten from your cottage is a lot of bear fur. No fingerprints other than yours and mine, no hairs except yours and mine...which by the way made my other two techs look at me with considerable interest.''

Tamara felt her cheeks grow hot. Everyone was probably speculating that she and Clay were lovers. She was surprised that the notion didn't upset her more.

''We do think that whoever vandalized the school and your cottage is definitely male, approximately between five foot ten to six feet tall.''

''How do you know that?'' she asked curiously.

''Logical deduction by where the claw marks were placed on the walls.'' He stood and walked over to the wall. ''The marks were about the same height wherever they were made.'' He raised an arm to its full extent. ''The pressure of the marks indicate his reach wasn't at its fullest extent when he made them. We've deduced his height by measuring those marks and the pressure used to make them.'' He dropped his hand to his side.

''That's amazing,'' she exclaimed and tried not to notice the width of his shoulders beneath his white T-shirt, shoulders she knew were warm, with supple skin pleasing to the touch.

It had been so long since she'd been held in big, strong arms, so long since she'd felt the touch of a man's hand on her body. She was hungry for physical contact, for the kind of intimacy that had been lacking in her life for the past two years.

''Have you ever looked at a hair beneath a microscope before?'' he asked.

''No. I'm afraid science and biology were never strong suits of mine.''

''Come here.'' He moved back to stand next to the microscope.

Heartbeat stepping up its rhythm, she got up from her chair and approached where he stood. She knew her heart wasn't racing at the anticipation of seeing a hair magnified. It was the crazy thrill she got by being near Clay.

She stepped close to him, so close she could feel the heat that radiated from his body, so close that when he turned to look at her she could feel the warmth of his breath on his face.

"And now we need a hair." He raised a hand and drew his fingers through her strands. His eyes were the ebony of the deepest shadows of night.

At the moment she was about to lean closer to him, he plucked a hair from her scalp. "Ouch!" she exclaimed and took a step back from him.

"Sorry. I thought it would be more interesting for you to see not only the hair, but the follicle as well."

She rubbed her head and eyed him balefully. "And what's wrong with seeing your follicle?"

He grinned, that charming expression that threatened to buckle her knees. "I've already seen my own, but I haven't seen yours."

He pulled open a drawer in the stainless steel table and took out the items he needed to mount the hair on a slide. She moved closer, watching him with interest, noting that his slender fingers moved with efficiency and grace.

"There we go," he said and put the slide into place. He peered into the eyepiece and twisted several knobs, then grunted as if in satisfaction.

He moved aside and motioned her to take a look. She looked at the magnified hair, but all her consciousness was focused on Clay, who stood next to her and had placed a hand on her shoulder.

His hand was hot against her bare skin and she felt electrified at every point of bodily contact.

"We can tell a lot by examining hairs," he said softly. The words were whispered into her ear as if they were a lover's secret.

"We can tell nationality and whether the hair had been color treated or not," he continued. "And if we have the hair follicle we can extract DNA."

"Fascinating." The single word came with difficulty from her. She felt breathless, as if his nearness was stealing all the oxygen meant for her.

She looked up at him and saw that his onyx eyes blazed with a fire that seemed to consume her.

For a long breathless minute neither of them moved. She was held captive by the desire that burned so bright in his eyes, a desire that evoked all the yearnings she'd tamped down for the past three days.

"Clay…" His name fell from her trembling lips. She wasn't sure if it was an entreaty or an unconscious desire to break the sensual net that was slowly entrapping her.

He held her gaze for another long moment, then stepped back from her. "There's nothing more I'd like to do right now than kiss you senseless. But if I take you into my arms, I won't want to stop at kisses."

"If you take me into your arms, I'm not sure I'd want you to stop at kisses."

The flames in his eyes intensified, but he didn't move. "I want you to be sure, Tamara. I want you to be absolutely certain that you understand that I'm offering you nothing more than a moment of passion. I don't want there to be any pretenses, any regrets or recriminations."

He took another step away from her. ''I'm going to go take a shower. The ball is in your court, Tamara. I won't pressure you either way.'' With these words he turned on his heels and disappeared down the hallway.

Tamara remained frozen in place, every nerve ending tingling in her body in response to his words. Physically, he hadn't touched her, but her body felt as if heated hands had stroked it. Rapid breathing accompanied a sweet rush of anticipation.

''The ball is in your court, Tamara.'' His words replayed in her head. The problem was she didn't know if she should pass it away or grab it and run all the way.

Chapter 11

Clay stood beneath the lukewarm water and hoped it would cool his blood. He'd known the moment was approaching when he would no longer be able to keep his lust for Tamara in check.

He'd even found it difficult to concentrate at work knowing that she was in his home. The past two evenings he'd come home from work indecently early, a definite break from his usual routine.

One thing he had discovered was that the peace and tranquility he'd felt when he'd been at Tamara's place hadn't come from the cottage and the setting, but rather from the woman herself.

There was an air of quiet confidence about her, a calm acceptance of who she was in heart and soul.

Her aura had taken over his home and for the first time since he'd bought the house he didn't mind spending time here. Even though she'd brought a sense of peace to the house, she'd also brought a new kind of tension to him—a sexual awareness he hadn't felt for a very long time.

He grabbed a bar of minty soap and soaped himself from head to toe. Surely he'd scared her off with his unvarnished version of what she could expect from him. He'd been quite clear so there wouldn't be room for any misunderstandings. He offered her nothing more than his passion, nothing more than his body.

Tamara was probably now hiding in her room like a timid virgin. If she was smart that's exactly where she would remain, at least for the remainder of this night.

He stepped out of the shower and grabbed the towel he'd laid out before getting beneath the spray. At least they didn't have to share a bathroom. She had the hall guest bath and he had his own off the master bedroom.

Things would have been far more difficult if they'd had to share the personal space of a bathroom.

He dried off, then wrapped the damp towel around his waist and started out of the bathroom, but froze in the doorway. Tamara was not only in his bedroom, but sat on his bed, clad in her yellow nightgown and robe.

The shower he'd just taken in an effort to ease his raging hormones was instantly rendered ineffectual. The sight of her electrified his entire body. The blood that had cooled instantly fired through his veins. "I told you what would happen the next time you wore those things," he said, his voice husky with his desire.

"Yes, you did." She stood from the bed and took a step toward him. That's all he needed. In three long strides he was in front of her. He gathered her in his arms as his mouth took possession of hers.

She met him eagerly, her lips instantly parting for him. Her arms rose to twine around his neck and he pulled her toward him so they were pressed intimately close…chests, hips and thighs.

Blood surged inside him as he felt her taut nipples against his chest, the heat of her center against his arousal, the feel of her warm skin beneath his fingertips.

Her kiss was as wild and unrestrained as his and her tongue met his with an eager hunger that matched his own. The taste of her mouth was tantalizing and flavored with uncontrollable want.

He raked his hands up and down her back, the material of the robe slick and silky. But he didn't want to feel her robe. He wanted to feel the silk of her skin.

With their mouths still locked together in a breathless kiss, he shoved the robe from her shoulders and it fell to the floor behind her. He slid his hands over her shoulders, her skin as soft, as satiny as he'd imagined.

He broke their kiss and stepped back from her, wanting to see her in the scrap of silk he'd been fantasizing about since the moment he'd seen it thrown across her bed.

Just as he'd imagined, the bright yellow silk was in beautiful contrast to her dusky skin tones. Her nipples showed through the thin material. Dark and erect, they beckoned his hands forward with the need to touch…to caress.

As he covered her breasts with his hands and

flicked his thumbs across her turgid nipples, a soft moan of pleasure escaped her.

The sound sent an electric jolt through him and once again he grabbed her to him and tangled his hands in the length of her hair.

''For the last two nights all I've been able to do is think about you in that nightgown…think about you out of that nightgown.'' As he spoke, his mouth moved down her jawline, nipping lightly at the sweet-scented tender skin of her neck and throat.

She dropped her head back to allow him access to the secret hollows and sensitive skin. The obvious acquiescence of the action torched his desire for her to a higher degree.

He felt as if all his civilized manners were burning away, leaving the primal need to rip the nightgown from her body, throw her on his bed and take complete and utter possession of her.

His mouth moved across the smooth skin of her shoulder as his hands once again cupped her breasts through the gown. Her hands were no less busy… running across the width of his back, teasingly touching his waist just above where the towel hung precariously around his hips.

Each touch of her fingers threatened to snap what little control he had left. He couldn't ever remember wanting another woman as badly as he wanted her. He couldn't ever remember feeling the intense need he felt right now.

Surprised to find his fingers trembling, he reached up and slid the spaghetti straps from her shoulders. She shrugged her shoulders to aid him.

The yellow silk hung for just a moment against her full breasts, then tumbled to the floor, leaving her clad only in a transparent pair of panties that left nothing to his imagination.

The moment her nightgown left her body, she reached out and pulled the end of the towel that released the terry cloth and sent it to the floor as well.

They stood face-to-face, naked and proud, unselfconsciously eyeing each other with hunger. "Beautiful," he said.

"I feel beautiful when you look at me that way," she replied. She slid two fingers beneath the waist of the panties and drew them slowly down over her hips and down her shapely thighs. When they reached the floor she stepped out of them and took a step closer to the bed.

The inertia that had momentarily gripped him snapped and once again he reached for her, this time tumbling them both onto his bed as his mouth ravished hers. He couldn't get enough of her…the taste of her…the feel of her as their bodies entwined.

Don't rush…don't rush, a little voice whispered in his head. Somewhere in a place where common sense still reined, he knew this was in all probability a one-time, one-night-stand kind of thing. He wanted it to be an experience she would never forget.

Once again he claimed her mouth, at the same time his hands moved over her breasts, teasing the taut tips as she moaned her pleasure.

He replaced his hands with his mouth, licking and biting lightly at her nipples as her hands tangled in his hair, then scratched lightly across his shoulders.

As he loved her breasts with his mouth, his hands slid across her flat abdomen, down her hips and across the sensitive area of her inner thigh. She responded to his touch, moving her hips in a rhythm as ageless as time itself.

He stroked her thighs, her hips, her lower abdomen, but didn't touch her intimately. He wanted her gasping with want...desperate with need.

When she reached down to grasp him in her hand, he caught her wrist and gazed at her. "Not yet," he whispered, reveling in the glaze that had descended over her eyes...the glaze of sheer pleasurable sensation.

He didn't want her to touch him yet. He knew that with her first touch he'd lose what little control he was desperately trying to maintain.

Again he raked his fingers along her inner thighs, stopping just short of where he knew she needed his touch most of all.

"You're torturing me." The words came from her as a whispered gasp.

"I know. I want you desperate for me."

She laughed and half sobbed at the same time. "I am desperate for you."

He laughed, but the laughter swiftly died as he captured her lips once again. At the same time his fingers touched the moist cleft between her thighs.

She gasped against his mouth as he moved his fingers against her, stroking her where he knew all her nerves were centered.

She arched to meet him, thrashing against the bed as her body grew taut with tension. Her fingers gripped the sheets on either side of her as he continued a rhythm intended to drive her over the edge.

He'd never been as aroused as he was at this moment, watching her as the waves of pleasure swept through her. She cried out and stiffened and he knew she was there, drowning in the waves.

Her entire body went limp and her eyes flickered open and held his gaze. Not saying a word, she reached down and encircled his arousal with her hand. The feel of her fingers wrapped firmly around him caused his breath to catch painfully in his chest.

A voracious need filled him as her fingers stroked lightly up and down the length of him. He needed to be inside her now, feeling her velvety depths surrounding him.

With a groan, he moved away from her and reached into his nightstand. He withdrew one of the foil wrappers. Even though he was half-mindless with passion, he wasn't stupid.

She surprised him by taking the package from him. She ripped it open, then withdrew the condom from inside. She pushed him so that he was on his back, then she kissed each of his flat male nipples as her hair caressed his chest.

The raw sensuality she exuded made him feel as if he were about to explode. He groaned again and she raised her head and smiled at him, her eyes sparking with pleasure. Again she licked and kissed his nipples, then moved her mouth down his chest, down his abdomen, stopping just short of touching his erection.

This time his groan was louder, a savage expression of the intense need that ripped up from deep inside him. He froze as she took the condom and slid it over the tip of him. Slowly she rolled it down his erect length, then encircled him once again with her hand.

He grabbed her hand to keep it still, knowing that if she stroked him he would lose all control. "Now you're torturing me.'' His voice was so raspy, so guttural he scarcely recognized it as his own.

''I know. I want you desperate for me,'' she said, repeating back to him his own words.

''I am desperate for you,'' he said and rolled her over on her back. Poised above her, he watched her eyes as he slid into her. Dark and filled with emotion, they held his gaze, then flickered closed as a moan escaped her lips.

Buried inside her, he remained still for a long moment, the sensation of her warmth overwhelming him. He fought for control, but as she raised her knees to allow him greater depth, the last modicum of control shattered.

They moved together in a frenzy, meeting each other thrust for thrust. He was vaguely aware of her crying his name over and over again as he continued to plunge into her.

He felt the tension once again building in her, knew by the rake of her fingers against his back and the wildness of her movements that she was about to reach the pinnacle once again.

He increased his rhythm, wanting her, needing her to get there before he did and he was perilously close. As she tightened her thighs around him and cried out once again, he felt the tremors that shook her body. That was all it took for him to fall into his own spiral of release.

They made love once more before he fell asleep, his arms wrapped tightly around her, his body pressed intimately against her own.

She couldn't sleep. She was flooded with emotions too enormous to allow slumber. Nothing she had ever experienced with Max had come close to the mind-shattering pleasure of Clay's lovemaking. Nothing in her wildest imagination had come close to conceiving mentally the heights of splendor that were possible when making love.

In this, he'd been her warrior—in control, sure of himself and commanding. He'd also been gentle and tender and had caused her to respond to him not only physically, but emotionally as well.

She knew better than to read anything special into what they'd just shared. It had been an explosion of physical desire for him, nothing more, nothing less.

He'd told her exactly what he was offering before she'd come into his bedroom. And even knowing that emotionally he'd been offering little, she hadn't been able to stop herself from going to him.

"Tell me why the hummingbird is your totem."

His voice in the darkness of the night surprised her. She thought he was sleeping. She raised her head so she could look at him, loving the way the moonlight filtering in through the window caressed his relaxed features.

"The hummingbird seeks out the nectar of life by only going to the sweetness and beauty each flower offers. That's what I've always tried to do...to see the beauty, to look for the good in everything and everyone. The hummingbird struck a chord in me from a very early age and I embraced it as my totem." She hesitated a moment, then asked. "What about you? What's your totem animal?"

"It doesn't matter. I don't believe in that stuff." His hand stroked her hip. He lay on his back, an arm around her as she lay on her side with her hand on his chest. She could see in the moonlight that he was staring up at the ceiling.

"Okay, you don't believe in it, but I'd still like to know what your totem animal was when you did believe."

He finally moved his head slightly so he looked at her. "I was born at home and my mother always told me that my totem was the raccoon. She said that moments after I was born four raccoons came up to the bedroom window and peered inside and she knew then that the raccoon would be my totem."

She smiled. "The raccoon is a good totem. They're known for being intelligent and cunning and great protectors." Her smile faded. "Why did you stop believing, Clay? Why did you decide to reject being Native?" She held her breath, afraid that her questions might anger him.

He once again focused his gaze on the ceiling above them. His hand continued to caress her naked hip as a deep sigh escaped him. "I was ten years old when my mother opened the doors to the cultural center for the first time. For several years before that she'd been busy in the planning stages, getting funding, looking at blueprints, sharing her vision with anyone who would listen. There were times I thought that the cultural center was like a bothersome, time-consuming sibling."

"You were jealous of it?" she asked.

He bunched his pillow beneath his head so he was sitting up just a bit instead of lying flat. "Sure, but you know my mother, it was impossible not to get caught up in the excitement of it all."

Tamara smiled as she thought of his mother. Rita

was passionate in her love of her heritage and her need to share it and educate others.

"What a lot of people don't know is how much opposition she faced in what she was trying to do," he continued. "Most people still believed we belonged on reservations trading horses and drinking whisky."

She crossed her arms on his chest and rested her chin on top, enjoying the rumble of his voice, the warmth of his skin against hers. "But your mother was determined."

He smiled. "She was like a dog with a bone. The more people told her it would never happen, the more determined she was to make it happen." His smile fell and instead his features tensed.

She reached a hand out and stroked it down his strong jaw. "You'll find her, Clay. I know you will. You're like the raccoon…intelligent and cunning and you have great hunting powers."

He looked as if he were about to protest, then simply sighed again. "I was thirteen years old when I decided I didn't want to be Native anymore," he continued.

"Why? What happened?"

"Every weekend Mom dragged me to the cultural center to participate in something. At the same time I was also on the junior high school football team. One Sunday afternoon I was dancing at the cultural center when I looked out in the audience and saw the football team members there."

Tamara saw what was coming. She knew the cruelty of children and how sharp the gibes of taunting could jab. She had experienced some of it herself when she'd been young.

"They were laughing," he continued. "Laughing and pointing at me and I was mortified. For the next two weeks at school they tormented me, calling me dancing Indian boy, decorating my locker with feathers and beads. I told my mother I would never participate at the cultural center again and I quit the football team."

"Kids can be very mean." She had a feeling there was more to the story, but she was afraid to press him. Childish taunts from silly kids wouldn't be enough to make a man hate his roots, hate the very essence of who he was.

She wanted to ask more questions, but was afraid. She didn't know if it was the darkness of the room that had allowed him to let down his guard and share just a little bit of himself, or the fact that they'd been intimate with each other.

"Yeah, there are a lot of mean people in the world. That's why I like doing what I do...helping put mean people behind bars."

"Are you good at what you do?"

"As good as I can be with the equipment I have. I'd love to work at one of the labs they show on those television shows. They have workspace and equipment that I can only dream about. Too much of the physical evidence I get has to be sent away to Oklahoma City for testing."

"But surely there are a lot of preliminary things you can do."

"Sure." He frowned. "But so far my work hasn't yielded results in the cases that are most important."

She flattened her hands and kissed his chest. "You'll find her, Clay."

"It's not just my mother I'm worried about. The

person who killed Greg Maxwell and Sam McClane is still out there and nobody knows when another murder will occur.'' His hand caressed up from her hip and along the side of her breast. ''And then there's you.''

His warm hand made it difficult for her to concentrate on anything else. ''You don't have to worry about me,'' she replied with effort. ''I still think the vandalism is the work of a student, but none of them are crazy enough to play the legend out to the end.''

''It's pretty damn crazy to take bear claws and mark up rooms with deer blood,'' he countered. He turned on his side so he was facing her. ''And what's craziest of all is that I want you again.''

''That doesn't sound crazy at all to me,'' she said, half-breathlessly, then went willingly into his arms as his lips met hers in a kiss that left no doubt of the desire that burned through them both.

Dawn was just breaking when the ringing of the phone awakened them. Clay sat up and fumbled for the phone on the nightstand, as alert as if he'd been waiting for the call. Tamara sat up as well, knowing that a dawn phone call could only mean trouble.

''I'm on my way,'' Clay said after listening for only a moment. He hung up the phone and was out of the bed at the same time. ''Go back to sleep,'' he said to her as he pulled on a pair of jeans. ''It's still early.''

''What's happened?'' she asked.

''There's been another murder.'' He pulled a T-shirt over his head. ''I'll call you when I get a chance. In the meantime don't open the door for anyone.'' With these final words he left the room.

Another murder. Tamara sat up and swung her feet over the side of the bed. It was so difficult to imagine that while she and Clay had made love, while they had shared in the beauty of the physical give and take, somebody evil had been taking the life of another.

Chapter 12

As Clay drove toward the center of town where Glen Cleberg had told him the body had been found, he went over the checklist of his job in his head. Approach scene. Secure and protect scene. Preliminary survey. Evaluate physical evidence possibilities. Photograph scene. Sketch scene. Detailed search and record and collection of physical evidence. Final survey.

He knew his job as well as he knew the beat of his own heart, but he needed to focus on something other than the warm, sweet woman who had been in his arms throughout the night.

Still, even knowing he was headed to a horrible crime scene, his mind couldn't release the memories of the night he'd just shared with Tamara. He'd known instinctively that she'd be passionate, but he hadn't expected the intense passion she'd shown.

He'd known instinctively that she would be gentle and tender, but he hadn't expected those traits to be tempered with a teasing sensuality that had driven him half-mad.

Almost as good as the sex had been the way their bodies had fit together so neatly as they'd slept. It was as if each had been made specifically for the other.

He'd felt a peace that he hadn't felt for as long as he could remember and for just a moment it seemed as if everything was right in the world.

He frowned and shoved these thoughts away, knowing he'd need all his concentration for what lie ahead. Besides, everything wasn't right with the world. He was headed to a murder scene and his mother was still missing. And there was no way in hell he would ever be the kind of man Tamara wanted and needed in her life.

Glen had given him precious little information, only that Tim O'Brien had been found naked and dead and on the sidewalk in front of the hardware store.

Clay didn't know Tim O'Brien well, although he'd seen him around town and knew he owned a real estate office. He'd been a good-looking man in his late thirties. And now, from what Glen had told Clay, he was the third victim of the Shameless Slasher.

"Dammit." Clay hit the dashboard with the palm of his hand, frustration eating at his insides. He could only hope that this time the killer had gotten sloppy and had left something behind...something that could point to a positive identification.

He saw the scene ahead when he was still a block away. Police cars were parked in the street and yellow tape shone in the dawn light, strung to protect and secure the area.

The crime-scene van was already there and he knew his partners, Trey and Burt were awaiting his arrival and instructions.

Preliminary survey, he told himself as he parked his car, grabbed his case and headed toward the scene. As he approached, his gaze swept the area before him, looking for anything that might appear out of place. Clues could often be found outside the secured area.

Trey met him near the scene. ''Hell of a way to wake up,'' he said.

''You're telling me,'' Clay agreed. ''What have you got so far?''

''Jason Sheller was the first officer on the scene. He said he was doing a drive-by, spied the body and immediately recognized what we had. He called it in and the chief instructed him to secure the area and not let anyone around until you got here.''

''Good, so the scene has been contained.''

''As far as I know nobody has gone inside the tape except the medical examiner who pronounced the victim dead.''

''Time of death?'' Clay asked as the two men approached the crime-scene tape where Burt stood waiting for them.

''According to the lividity and temperature of the body and the state of rigor mortis, he's saying that he's been dead between five and seven hours.''

Clay frowned. Too long for a body left out in the open. There already could be all kinds of airborne contaminants obscuring or confusing real evidence.

He stopped just outside of the taped-off area and looked around. He knew how important it was to get a complete mental picture not only of the victim, but also of the surrounding area in order to properly process the scene.

It was a tough transition, from Tamara's warm arms and his peaceful sleep to this vision of murder. Tim O'Brien was on his back on the sidewalk, his nakedness looking as obscene as anything Clay had ever seen as the pinkish light of dawn played over the body.

The only thing more obscene than the stark nakedness of the body was the blood that decorated his chest and stomach from the multiple stab wounds he'd received.

"There's no doubt it's one of the slasher's," Burt said. "It's exactly the same M.O. and the signature of leaving the victim naked and out in a public area. I'm sure the wounds will show the same type of knife used in this one as the last two."

"We might as well get started," Clay said. The three men opened their cases and began to put on gloves and plastic footies.

As they were doing this, Chief Cleberg hurried over to Clay. He looked older than his years, harassed half-mindless, and he pulled Clay away from the other two men and leaned toward him conspiratorially.

"You've got to find something, Clay. You've got to find something to catch this madman. People are starting to panic and I don't have anything to tell them to reassure them."

"I'll do my best, Chief, but so far this creep hasn't left anything behind for us to work with."

"There's got to be something. Whoever is doing this has to be stopped." A wildness possessed Glen's eyes and the redness of his neck and face made Clay fear the man was on the verge of a stroke.

"Go home, Glen," Clay said. "There's nothing you can do here. Let me and my men do what you pay us to do. I'll call you if we get anything to go on."

Glen sighed and raked a hand through his thinning hair. "You sure you have things under control here?" It was obvious he'd rather be anywhere than here with the latest victim.

"Just leave me a couple of patrolmen to keep the gawkers away and maintain the integrity of the site, and I'll keep you posted."

In truth, Clay would prefer Glen not be on site. It was much easier for Clay and his men to do their jobs without the chief looking over their shoulders.

He breathed a sigh of relief as Glen nodded, bellowed several orders, and then headed for his car. Clay turned to Trey and Burt. "Let's get going. Hopefully we can finish up here before the morning crowd starts heading into town."

His hope to finish up before the streets filled with morning workers and traffic was short-lived. They had only managed to take photographs and draw diagrams before the first curiosity seekers began to crowd around the crime scene.

Clay released the body to the medical examiner as quickly as possible, not wanting Tim O'Brien, even in death, to suffer the indignity of his neighbors and friends seeing him naked in the morning sun.

Not only did they vacuum, bindle, collect and categorize each and every item that might have evidentiary value, Clay also studied the scene itself, trying to visualize how it all had played out.

As with the other two scenes, Tim's clothes were found near the body. They were bloodstained and folded neatly. The bloodstains indicated that Tim had been stabbed while dressed, then stripped naked after his death.

Why would a murderer take the time to strip the victims if not for the sheer humiliation of them? And how arrogant and in control he must feel as he took the time to strip the bodies.

There was a massive quantity of blood and Clay knew there was no way the murderer had walked away from this scene without Tim's blood on him.

Unfortunately, the laws wouldn't allow him to search each and every house in Cherokee Corners to see who might have bloody clothes hidden away somewhere. If the laws had provided such action, long ago Clay would have done a house-to-house search for his mother.

He couldn't think about her now. Nor could he entertain thoughts of Tamara, although thoughts about her continued to intrude. He had to stay focused on the here and now, on the dead body before him and the clues the scene might provide.

Unlike at the other two scenes, a footprint had been left in Tim's blood. The sight of that footprint exhilarated Clay. Finally. Something left behind.

He photographed the footprint from half a dozen angles, then carefully transferred the print so that it could be used later to identify the type and size of shoe that had made it. At first glance it looked to have been made by a man's sneaker...around a size nine or ten, but he wouldn't know for sure until he got it back to the lab and did some comparison studies.

Jason Sheller hovered nearby, watching everything

that was being collected, coming precariously close to running the risk of contaminating things as he crowded too near. "Why don't you go canvass the area and see if anyone saw anything," Clay finally said when Jason got too close to what he was doing.

"Two men are already doing that," Jason replied. "What have you found so far?"

Clay looked at Jason, surprised to see a tinge of fear in Jason's eyes. "I won't know for sure what I've found until we get everything back to the lab and sort it all out. But you know that, Sheller, so what's up?"

"Nothing's up. What could be up with me? I'm just curious, that's all. I'm allowed to be curious, aren't I?" He turned and walked away, leaving Clay staring at his back. What had that been all about?

Clay returned his focus to his work, but his mind replayed the small exchange with Jason. There had been defensiveness in his tone and fear darkening his eyes.

Maybe it was because Jason usually worked the night shift and had been the one to find Tim this morning. Maybe he was afraid of becoming the next victim.

Clay sighed in frustration. If he could just do his job right and find the killer, then nobody in his town would have to be afraid again.

Tamara had thought she would get up the moment Clay had left. But after a moment of hesitation, she'd curled back up in the bed, this time on his side, where his scent was strongest and the bedding still retained his body heat.

She must have fallen back asleep for when she

opened her eyes again, the sun was fully up. She remained where she was, stretched out on Clay's side of the bed, his pillow beneath her head, and thought of the night that had passed.

He'd not only been a masterful lover, but he'd been passionate and emotional as well. For those moments of lovemaking, he'd owned her body, heart and soul.

However, as was always the case with the coming of dawn, morning regrets niggled in the back of her head as she got into the shower. She'd known when she'd gone to his room the night before that she was making a mistake, that making love with Clay would just make it more difficult to go back to her cottage and forget him.

He'd been quite clear what he was offering and there had been nothing in his words to give her any hope for anything other than what she'd received already from him…a night of splendid lovemaking.

The morning passed slowly, her thoughts consumed by Clay and the work he was involved in at the moment. Another murder. The pressure on him would be even more intense than it had been before.

She thought of the reason he'd given her for turning his back on his Native heritage. Cruel schoolmates, childish taunts and teasing, everyone at one time or another in their lives experienced such things.

She couldn't believe that what he'd shared with her had been the sum and total for his rejecting the Cherokee ways and teaching, for alienating himself from the cultural center that had meant so much to his mother and to the town itself. There had to be more. But apparently he hadn't been willing to share any more.

She had just sat down at the table for lunch when

she heard a noise coming from the front door. Instantly she froze with fear. She knew when Clay had left early that morning to process a crime scene that she probably wouldn't see him back home until late tonight.

Until this moment fear for her personal safety hadn't been an issue. Even though her cottage had been ripped apart, since she'd come here she hadn't given another thought to the fact that somebody might be after her.

What if the "bear" had found her? What if he had somehow discovered that she was staying here and knew that Clay was gone and she was all alone?

As noiseless as possible, she got up from the table and slid a butcher knife from the silverware drawer. She held it tight in her hand, out before her as a weapon, then crept from the kitchen and into the living room in time to see Breanna coming through the front door.

Breanna squealed in surprise at the sight of her. "You scared me to death," she exclaimed.

"You scared me, too," Tamara replied as she quickly put the knife down on the end table between the two chairs.

"What are you doing here?" Breanna asked. Tamara followed her as she carried a covered dish through the living room and into the kitchen.

"I'm staying here for a couple of days."

Breanna eyed her with obvious curiosity. "Really? Clay didn't mention a thing about having a house-guest." She placed the dish on the table. "I heard there was another murder and knew he'd be busy all day. I fixed him a casserole because I know he never eats well when he's in the middle of a case." She smiled at Tamara slyly. "It never occurred to me he might have a woman here cooking for him."

"I'm just here until Jeb can clean up the mess at my cottage," Tamara explained. "Alyssa was all booked up at the bed-and-breakfast so Clay invited me to stay here."

"Really?" Breanna sat at the table, obviously in no hurry to leave.

"Uh...I was just about to have a tuna sandwich. Would you like to join me?"

"I'd love to."

Surprised, Tamara got up and made an additional sandwich then returned to the table. She and Breanna weren't what she would consider friends. They had seen each other often at the cultural center and had always exchanged cheerful pleasantries, but they'd never shared any real time together.

"So, Clay invited you to stay here. That's very interesting. Most of the time Clay is so antisocial, he doesn't even invite any of his family members here. Very interesting." She looked at Tamara as if she was a new breed of insect.

"I understand there's going to be a new member to your family," Tamara said in an effort to change the focus off herself and Clay.

"Yes." Breanna touched her stomach, a smile curving her lips. "Adam and I are thrilled, and of course Maggie has already planned her baby brother's entire life."

"Brother? You already know it's a boy?"

"No, but Maggie is certain it is."

"I wish you all the best," Tamara said, a wistfulness welling up inside her. What would it be like to carry a baby inside her? What could it be like to carry Clay's baby?

"There's only one thing that can make everything perfect and that's if my mother is with me when I deliver this baby." The happiness that had shone in her eyes was doused, replaced by the sadness of her mother's absence.

"She'll be there," Tamara said with as much conviction as she could muster.

"Of course she will," Breanna agreed, but both women recognized that with each day that passed, the odds grew worse and worse that Rita would be returned home safe and sound.

For a moment the two were silent, then Breanna cast Tamara another sly grin. "So, tell me what, exactly, is going on between you and my brother."

Had she been asked the question yesterday, the answer would have been easier. As it was, she felt the warmth that swept through her body, up her neck and over her face and knew it was impossible that Breanna would miss the blush.

"I told you, he's just been kind enough to let me stay here until my place is back in order."

Breanna grinned. "I've known my brother all my life and he's never kind unless there's something in it for him."

Tamara laughed. "What an awful thing to say."

"It was, wasn't it. What I mean is Clay would give any of us the shirt off his back if we needed it. But he's never been very open to other people." Breanna took a bite of her sandwich, her gaze lingering and speculative on Tamara. "You're in love with him."

Tamara's bite of sandwich stuck in her throat at the

unexpectedness of the statement. For a moment she had no idea how to answer.

"Your cousin Alyssa warned me that the worst thing I could do would be to fall in love with your brother."

Breanna smiled once again. "Alyssa and Clay often butt heads. Alyssa thinks Clay is hardheaded and hard-hearted. Clay thinks Alyssa is too soft-hearted and hardheaded."

"And Clay isn't hardheaded and hard-hearted?" Tamara asked.

"Of course he is. He's a man, isn't he?" Breanna laughed. "He's stubborn and can be brusque to the point of rudeness. He's single-minded and obsessed with his work. But if you could see him for ten minutes with my daughter, Maggie, you'd know that there's so much more to him than that."

"I already know that," Tamara said softly. She remembered the tenderness that Clay had exhibited the night before as he'd held her in his arms, stroked her hip as they had whispered in the darkness of the night.

"You're in love with him." It was more question than statement but Breanna didn't wait for her reply. "Tamara, he can be a hard man, a difficult man, but if you can get beneath his defenses, if you can get him to open up his heart to you, then I say go for it. He needs somebody…something good in his life that is all his own."

Long after Breanna had left, her words replayed in Tamara's head. He needed somebody in his life. He needed something good in his life. But could he ever open up his heart to accept something good, someone special? And could she be the woman to do that?

The bigger question was did she want to be the

woman to do that. She left the kitchen and went into the living room where her mother and father's broken courting flute was on a shelf next to Clay's worktable.

She picked up one of the pieces, running her hands over the smooth wood that had been delicately carved. The courting flute was one of the Cherokee traditions, part of what she'd seen for herself in her visions of her future.

If she did manage to get beneath Clay's defenses, if he fell in love with her and decided he wanted to build a future with her, then she'd have to figure out if she was willing to sacrifice all that she'd once dreamed about marriage and her spirit mate.

But the main thing she wondered about was if Clay was truly a man who had turned his back on his blood—on his heritage—or if he was a wounded warrior who needed somebody to help him to find his way back home.

Chapter 13

For the next three days work consumed Clay. All his focus, all his energy, was directed at trying to find something in the evidence that had been gathered at the latest murder scene.

He spent his days running tests, doing comparisons and packaging items to be sent to the bigger lab in Oklahoma City. He marked the material as a priority, but knew not to expect results back too quickly.

He left the house before dawn each morning and rarely returned until after eleven or twelve at night. No matter what time he got home, Tamara was waiting up for him with a meal, a gentle smile and no expectations of conversation or anything else.

He'd left work earlier this evening, burnt out and exhausted. As he drove home, he was irritated to realize how much he looked forward to Tamara's presence in his house.

His house had come alive with her there. In some

cases her presence was subtle, the scent of her in the air, the life energy that had taken possession of the space.

In other cases, her presence was more overt. Wildflowers now filled the house, colorful, sweet-scented bouquets in water glasses. The place had begun to smell like a home instead of a house, the scents a combination of her perfume, good cooking and cleansers. Gone was the sterile environment he'd become accustomed to and it irritated him more than a little bit that he was growing far too accustomed to having her there.

He pulled up, unsurprised to see the porch light on, awaiting his arrival. He got out of his car, weariness weighing heavily on his shoulders…a weariness coupled with a growing irritation from an unknown source.

It was obvious she hadn't been expecting him so early. He unlocked the door, walked inside and found her sketching at the kitchen table.

"Clay!" She jumped up from the table at the sight of him and quickly turned her sketch pad over. "You're earlier than you've been the last couple of nights."

"Yeah, I decided I'd had enough of looking at pictures and test results of the aftermath of murder for one day."

"Sit down," she said as she got up from the table. "I've got your dinner in the microwave. It will just take a minute or two to heat up."

He started to protest, but instead sank down to the table. He hadn't eaten all day and even though he was feeling unusually irritable, that didn't mean he didn't need to eat.

He watched her as she got the meal ready. She was clad in some sort of baggy muumuu-like gown that covered her from neck to feet and obscured any hint of the curves beneath. And he found it sexy as hell. Maybe it was because he knew intimately what lay beneath the flowered material.

He hadn't touched her since the night they had made love, but that didn't mean he hadn't thought about it. Even though he'd come home each night beyond exhaustion, in those moments before falling asleep in his big, lonely bed, he'd thought about their night spent together.

The microwave dinged its completed heating as she set a glass of iced tea before him. "You know, you don't have to do this every night," he said as she placed the plate of chicken, rice and corn in front of him.

She sat across from him with a glass of tea for herself. "I really don't mind. There isn't much for me to do here, especially since I don't have my paints. Besides…" She smiled, the wide, generous smile that never failed to create a catch in his breathing. "Cooking for you seems to be the least I can do for your hospitality in letting me stay here."

She was too good to be true, he thought as he began to eat the meal she'd prepared. She was too centered, too generous, too easy-going and at peace with herself. He wasn't sure why, but something in his current mood made him want to pick a fight with her, see her peaceful tranquility shatter.

Instead he focused on the meal, knowing that the frustration he felt, the need to lash out at something or someone had nothing to do with her, but rather the feeling of inadequacy that gnawed at him concerning his work.

Still, the delicious meal did nothing to staunch the roiling emotions that threatened to explode inside him. The moment he finished eating, she reached for his plate but he stopped her by grabbing her wrist. "You aren't my maid, Tamara. I can put my own plate in the dishwasher."

Her eyes were huge as she gazed at him. "Okay," she said and pulled her wrist from his grip. She remained standing as if uncertain what to do next. "I'll just let you finish up here then." She picked up her sketch pad and pencils and left the kitchen.

A mixture of emotions sliced through him as he rinsed his plate and put it in the dishwasher, emotions he couldn't begin to name or even identify.

Maybe it was just a combination of exhaustion and frustration, and perhaps a bit of sexual want for the woman he shouldn't want.

He went into the living room where she was seated on one of the chairs. The television played softly, tuned to a popular sitcom. He sat in the other chair, staring unseeing at the television screen, too aware of her so close to him.

Closing his eyes, he rubbed his forehead in an attempt to dispel the visions of death that he'd viewed all day long. Greg Maxwell. Sam McClane. Tim O'Brien. He'd spent much of his day looking at the crime-scene photos, seeing those men naked and vulnerable in death.

"Clay? Are you all right? Do you have a headache?"

Her voice, so soft and solicitous both soothed and irritated at the same time. He dropped his hand from his forehead and looked at her. "No, I don't have a headache and no, I'm not all right."

"What's wrong?" Those beautiful gray eyes of hers were filled with concern. "What can I do to help?"

Her question made his irrational irritation rise to new heights. "What can you do to help?" He slid his gaze over her, pointedly lingering on the thrust of her breasts before returning to look her in the eyes. "You could take my mind off all my problems by going to bed with me."

She stood from her chair. "All right."

He stared at her in astonishment. "You'd do that? You'd let me use you like that?"

She smiled, a challenging grin that twinkled in her eyes. "What makes you think you'd be using me? Maybe I'd be using you."

A sharp burst of laughter flew from his lips. The laughter was unexpected and somehow tension relieving. "And just why would you want to use me by rolling around beneath the sheets with me?"

She shrugged. "Oh, I don't know…maybe because the television program that's playing now is a rerun and I'm going stir-crazy stuck in this house alone everyday and at least a roll between the sheets with you would maybe break the monotony somewhat."

She was calling his bluff and he knew it. And she knew that he knew it. "You might as well sit back down. I refuse to be used by a woman who only wants my body."

"You don't offer much else," she returned, still standing before him. "You don't share your thoughts, your feelings or anything else."

He frowned. "You don't want to hear my thoughts or know my feelings. They aren't worth sharing."

She kneeled down at his feet and placed her hands on his knees. Her gaze held his and he wanted to fall into the clear gray depths and stay there forever. "Clay, I know you don't like to talk about the sensitive matters of your ongoing cases. But I just want you to know that I'm here if you do want to talk about them…or anything else. I would consider anything you tell me a confidence, and I never break confidences."

She didn't need to tell him that. He trusted her implicitly. He reached out and stroked the length of her long, silky hair. She lay her head on his knees, as if to make it easier for him to run his fingers through the strands of hair.

He leaned his head back and closed his eyes, his fingers caressing as his body unwound from the taut knot it had been in for the past three days. One of her hands rubbed his knee, not in any sexual way, but rather in a soothing, soft rhythm.

"I'm afraid everyone has forgotten." As the words fell from his lips he raised his head and once again looked at her.

"Forgotten?"

"My mother." He frowned, a new knot forming in the center of his chest. "These murders that are taking place are terrible and I don't mean to take away from the importance of finding the person responsible and stopping them. But all the force is focused on that and everyone has stopped looking for Mom."

She grimaced and he realized he'd grabbed a handful of her hair too tightly. "I'm sorry," he said and quickly released his hold.

"It's all right." She propped her hands beneath her chin, her eyes filled with empathy. In that empathic look, his lips found words that had been aching inside him.

"I know it sounds crazy, but I'm so angry that these murders are happening now, that they take precedence over my missing mother. And when that anger comes upon me, it makes me feel childish. I mean, men are dying and all I want to do is get enough time to look at everything pertaining to my mother's case and solve it."

"I'm certainly no forensic scientist, but if there's anything I can do to help, just tell me," she offered.

He looked at her for a long moment, then indicated he wanted to get up. He stood, then took her hand and pulled her to her feet. "Let me show you something."

He walked over to his worktable and opened a drawer where he kept slides. He was intensely conscious of her nearness as he put the one he wanted under the microscopic eye. He focused it, then gestured for her to look at it. "Tell me what you see."

She lowered her head to peer into the eyepiece, then looked back at him with a frown. "They look like threads of some kind…blue threads."

He nodded. "They're a seventy-five percent polyester and twenty-five percent cotton blend."

"Where did you get them?"

"I found them stuck in the striker plate on the bedroom doorframe at my parents' house." He swiped a hand through his hair, exhausted, yet needing to talk about where he was on the case, talk about it to somebody who cared. "The problem is I don't know when they were left there or what they came from. I don't know it they're a clue or a piece of fluff that means nothing.''

"But at this point you can't dismiss anything, no matter how minute it might appear," she said.

"That's right."

She looked into the eyepiece again. "Did your mother have a dress that color? A blouse or something?"

"I don't think so." He'd thought about it over and over again since the moment he'd first seen those threads. "Mom didn't wear much blue, although she wore a lot of turquoise. I can't think of anything either her or Dad wore that would have caught on the striker plate and left those threads."

"Could it be from whoever came into your house that night and took your mother?" she asked.

"Could be…and maybe not." A new burst of frustration sliced through him. "At the moment it's all I've got…these blue threads and a handful of rocks."

"A handful of rocks?"

He told her about the Dalmatian blend of rocks that he had found both at the Frazier murder scene and in his mother and father's carpeting. "I've got copies of invoices from quarries and landscaping services around the state and I haven't even had a chance to go over them to see who might possibly be put on a suspect list."

"Do you have the invoices here? Clay, that's something I could do for you. I have hours here each day. At least I could help with this."

He hesitated only a moment, then reached back into the drawer and drew out a thick manila folder. "This is everything we have on the case. The invoices are in here, along with pictures, interviews and everything else. But you know you don't have to do this.''

''I know.'' She smiled, her eyes holding a touch of sadness. ''I miss her, too, Clay. Your mother welcomed me into the cultural center with open arms when I returned here from New York. With her friendship, her spirituality and her passion, she brought me back to who I needed to be.''

Clay realized at that moment that he'd needed to talk about his mother. He'd needed to hear somebody say good things about her, to know what a special person she was.

He stared down at the stainless steel worktable. ''You know, the last time I saw her I fought with her.'' The words squeezed out of him with a shaft of pain and unmitigated guilt. He turned his back to Tamara, the guilt ripping him up. ''I said some rotten things to her and the last look I saw on her face was pain and disappointment and it was all because of me.''

''Clay.'' Tamara touched his arm, but he didn't turn around. With a surprising strength, she grabbed his shoulder and forced him to turn and face her.

When he looked at her, her eyes swam with a mist of tears. She placed her cool, soft hands on either side of his face. ''You listen to me, Clay James. I don't know what you and your mother fought about and it doesn't really matter. Your mother talked about you every day that I saw her. She spoke of you with pride and love and nothing you could have said to her, nothing you could have fought about would have changed the fierce love she felt for you, the deep pride that burned in her heart for you.''

God, he'd needed to hear these words from somebody…anybody. Her words soothed the jagged edges that had existed in his heart since the moment of his mother's disappearance. He leaned his forehead against hers and closed his eyes. "Thank you," he said softly.

"Don't thank me. I didn't do anything but tell you the truth," she replied. "And you need to get some sleep. You've pushed yourself too hard in the last couple of days."

He raised his forehead from hers and looked at her intently. "Sleep with me, Tamara. I'm not asking for anything else. Just sleep with me tonight." He wanted her closeness, her warmth against him. Tonight he needed her beside him more than he'd ever needed anyone in his life.

Tamara knew when she agreed to sleep with him, that in all probability sleep would become something much more. It didn't matter that he was the wrong man for her, it didn't matter that there was no possible future between them. What mattered was the raw emotion that emanated from him, the need she saw in his eyes.

She was surprised when moments later they got into his bed and he pulled her into a warm embrace against him and promptly fell asleep.

She remained still, enjoying the feel of his strong arms around her, his toasty warm body with its masculine curvature against her back. At the same time she worried about him. What if they didn't ever find Rita?

She knew from their conversation earlier that it wasn't just grief that tore at his thoughts, but rather the burden of guilt as well. She had no idea what dynamics had been at play between mother and son, but she'd told him the truth about Rita's love and devotion to him, and his was obvious for her as well.

She didn't realize she'd drifted off to sleep until she came awake. She knew instinctively that she hadn't been sleeping very long and it took her only a moment to realize what had awakened her.

His hand cupped her breast and his lips nibbled on the back of her neck. "I thought I could do this," his voice whispered softly in her ear. "I thought I could have you here in my bed, sleeping next to me and not want you, but I was wrong."

Her heart kicked into a frantic beat as his fingers raked over the taut tip of her nipple. Even through the silk of her nightgown she could feel the heat of his hand, heat that beckoned her to burn with him.

She turned over to face him, his features barely discernable in the moonlight that seeped in through the window. "You should sleep. You need your rest."

She could see the smile that curved his lips as his hand once again swept over her throat, down her collarbones and over her breasts. "Is that a nice way of saying no?"

With his hands teasing her and that sexy smile riding his lips, the word "no" was no longer in her vocabulary. She ran her fingers across his broad chest. "Does this feel like no?" She leaned forward and kissed his neck, lingering in the dark hollow of his throat. "Or this?"

She had no opportunity to say another word. His mouth crashed to hers, her senses reeling, her breath half-stolen by the passionate ferocity of his kiss.

Within moments her nightgown was tossed to the

floor, as well as his boxers, and their naked bodies met in a frenzy of tangled flesh and beating hearts.

What had been his need became her own…the need to be joined with him, to meld into one. His tongue battled with hers as he stroked her naked flesh, creating a river of want splashing inside her.

Her hands were not idle. She loved the feel of his muscled chest and shoulders as well as his taut abdomen. The masculine scent of his cologne had become achingly familiar to her and swept her higher into the throes of desire.

Where before when they had made love it seemed as if they had indulged in foreplay for an eternity, this time they grappled each other hungrily, seeking union without the need for foreplay.

As he moved on top of her, poised between her thighs, love for him exploded inside her. She loved him with all her heart, all her soul. She loved the man he was and the man she knew he would become as years passed and wisdom grew.

She gasped his name as he entered her and her emotions rode so high tears sprang to her eyes. They were tears of joy mingling with tears of sorrow…sorrow that he could not be her future.

It didn't take long for the sorrow to diminish, overwhelmed by the joy of his deep thrusts inside her, his hungry kisses and his fiery touch. She gave herself to the joy, refusing to think of anything else but this moment with this man.

Afterward they lay in each other's arms, sated and waiting for sleep to come. "How come you teach the old legends?" he asked in a soft, half-sleepy voice. "I mean, why not just teach the history of the Cherokees?"

"I do teach a lot of history, but the legends are also a big part of our history. The legends tell about what kind of people we are…fun-loving and gentle and reverent of all life. The legends also teach morality and a variety of life lessons that are important."

"At the moment it seems one of your legends have only served to screw up your life," he said as his hand caressed her hair in a lulling rhythm.

"The legend didn't vandalize my classroom or my house. Somebody sick did that," she countered. "And that legend is one of the more important ones I teach. It's so important to remember the nature of all beasts and know that people and animals alike can't fight their nature."

She realized he'd fallen asleep, his hand had stopped moving in her hair and his breathing was deep and regular. The sorrow that had momentarily gripped her as they'd begun to make love returned. She closed her eyes against the tears that burned as she realized once again how much she loved the man who slept next to her.

He would never share her love for their heritage, he would never share her Cherokee pride. He would never carve her a courting flute or marry her in a traditional Cherokee wedding ceremony. They would never have children together and teach them to love and respect their Cherokee roots.

She squeezed her eyes more tightly closed to staunch the tears that tried to escape. There was only one thing more painful than not being loved at all, and that was loving a man who was absolutely, positively wrong for you.

Chapter 14

It had been another long day made longer by the fact that they were no closer to identifying the serial killer than they had been when the first body had been discovered.

But it wasn't thoughts of murder that played on Clay's mind as he drove toward home the next evening. It was thoughts of Tamara.

He was in love with her. He'd tried fighting it, tried ignoring it, but he couldn't any longer. Somehow, someway over the course of the last week, he'd fallen in love with her.

He didn't love her because of the fact that she cooked dinner for him each evening; he could easily hire somebody to do that. He loved sitting across from her at the table sharing tidbits of conversation as they ate whatever she had cooked.

He wasn't in love with her because they had great sex together. He could have picked up the phone and called half a dozen women who would have been more than willing to accommodate him on that score.

Maybe it was the way she tilted her head just slightly when she listened to him, or perhaps it was that smile that started in her eyes before taking full possession of her lips.

It was all the things that made her who she was— her pride, her inner serenity, her eye for beauty and strength. She'd told him she was like the hummingbird, seeking sweet nectar and the goodness of life. So, what had drawn her to him?

He was like an artificial flower, perhaps bright enough on the outside to draw a hummingbird, but holding no nectar, nothing that she could need or want.

He pulled up in front of his house, shut off his lights and engine, but remained in the car. What to do about Tamara? He knew she had feelings for him. It was in her eyes when she looked at him, in her touch and, like the song had said, definitely in her kiss.

It shouldn't be too long and Jeb would be letting her know that her cottage was once again habitable. There had been little time to work on the vandalism case so they still didn't know who was responsible and what kind of danger she still might be in. He knew she would insist on moving back to the cottage the moment it was ready.

One thing was certain. They couldn't go on the way they had been going. He didn't care how strong the temptation, he would not make love to her again. He couldn't. Eventually she would expect more and even though he might wish things could be different, he knew he had nothing more to give.

The front door opened and she stepped out on the porch. The hot night breeze plastered her sundress against her body, outlining each and every feature. He sighed. Catching a serial killer might be far easier than resisting the temptation of Tamara.

He got out of the car and ambled slowly toward the porch, unable to stop the slight catch of his heart as he approached her.

"You're earlier again tonight," she said. It was just before seven. "Did you eat?"

He nodded. He'd called her earlier in the day to tell her not to cook, that he was just going to grab a sandwich at work.

"I've got something to show you." With the guilelessness of a child, she took his hand in hers and led him through the living room and into the kitchen.

Papers lined the kitchen table in neat stacks. He saw the file on his mother's case there as well. "You've been busy," he said.

She flashed a quick smile. "I worked on this all day. I went through all the copies of invoices you'd received from the landscaping and quarries and made a list of people in and around Sycamore Ridge who have at one time or another ordered the Dalmatian blend of rocks." She held up a sheet of paper that appeared to have about ten names on it. "I think you'll find a surprise there."

He took the paper from her and quickly scanned the list. He sank into one of the chairs, for a moment speechless with shock. He looked up at Tamara. "Glen Cleberg? Are you sure about this?"

She nodded. "Three years ago he ordered a truckful of Dalmatian rock. The invoice shows it was delivered to his home address."

Clay felt as if he'd been kicked in the gut by a wild mustang. He stared down at the name once again. Chief Cleberg? "There was always a bit of bad blood between Glen and my father, but I can't imagine that Glen would have had anything to do with what happened out at my parents' house that night." He shot her a wry, humorless smile. "It's just not in his nature." Although, Clay intended to speak to Glen about it.

"All right, then what about the other names. Do any of them ring a bell?"

He scanned the list again. "Most of them are familiar, but none of them were friends or more than nodding acquaintances with my parents. No red flags that I can see here."

Tamara sighed with obvious disappointment. "I was hoping to help."

"You did help," he assured her. "You saved me hours of work by doing this."

"I did think of something else." She opened the file folder that held the photos of his parents' house. Some of the photos were quite grim…the ones of the chair where his father had been sitting when he'd been attacked, the blood spatter evidence that had arced on the walls from the blow Thomas had received to the back of his head.

She shuffled through these and came to a photo of his parents' bedroom. "The bedspread." She said the two words as if they should mean something to him as she shoved the picture in front of him.

"Yeah, what about it?"

"Look at it, Clay. It looks like it's the same color as those threads you found."

"How did I miss something so obvious?" His question was directed more to himself than to her.

"Maybe because it was so obvious and because you've probably seen that spread a hundred times in your life." She sat in the chair next to his. "I know it doesn't get you any closer to finding your mom, but at least it maybe solves the mystery of those threads. Maybe your mom caught it on the striker plate the last time she took it from the bedroom into the laundry room."

"Maybe." He frowned thoughtfully. "But I can't imagine her getting it caught then pulling hard enough to tear it. She loved that spread...loves that spread." It horrified him that it was beginning to get easier and easier to think about and talk about his mother in the past tense.

"It just doesn't quite feel right to me." He stood. "Maybe I'll take a drive over to the house and get the spread, check and see if I can find where the threads have been torn."

She stood as well. "Do you mind if I come with you? I've been cooped up here for a little over a week. I wouldn't mind a little fresh air."

He hadn't thought about what it must be like for her, stuck in this house all day and all night long. "Sure, take the ride with me."

Within minutes they were in the car and headed toward Clay's parents' farmhouse. Although the evening was quite warm, Tamara insisted she preferred the windows open to the air conditioner.

"I'm sorry, I hadn't thought about how difficult it was for you to spend hours and hours in the house without a break away," he said.

She smiled and waved her hand as if to forget the

whole subject. "It hasn't been a big deal. I just felt like some fresh air tonight."

They drove in silence, the comfortable quiet of two people in sync with one another. She was the first woman he'd ever spent any time with who didn't seem to be intimidated or worried about silence. Certainly his mother and his sisters had never met a silence they didn't want to break.

"Thanks for all the work you did today," he finally said.

"I didn't mind. I'd do anything I could to help you find her. She is somebody special to me, too."

She seemed to have no problem referring to his mother in the present tense and for that he was grateful. It didn't take them long to reach the ranch house.

He parked out front and steeled himself for seeing Uncle Sammy again. He hadn't seen him since the night he'd discovered his uncle had pawned his mother's jewelry. His anger had faded away with time…time to reflect that he shouldn't have been so surprised. After all, he knew his uncle's true nature and the act of pawning the jewelry had simply been a behavior of Sammy's nature.

"Have you ever met my father?" he asked as he shut off the engine.

"Yes, a couple of times at the cultural center."

"Why don't you come in with me and say hello. It would be good for Dad to see a familiar face that isn't family."

"All right," she agreed.

Together they walked up to the house where Clay knocked twice on the door then pushed it open and ushered Tamara inside. Sammy sat in a chair in front of the television and Thomas was on the sofa. Both men rose as Clay and Tamara entered.

Clay introduced Tamara to his uncle, then she and his father hugged. "I'll put some coffee on," Sammy said.

"No, that's all right. We aren't staying," Clay said. He turned to his father, who had sank back down on the sofa. "Dad, I'd like to take your bedspread back to my place."

Thomas frowned at him in bewilderment. "Why would you want to take the spread?"

"Let's just say I want to satisfy my curiosity about something," Clay replied. "It's probably no big deal, but it's something that's bugging me."

Thomas held his son's gaze for a moment, then waved a hand and sighed with the weariness of a man who had lost all hope. "Take whatever you want."

Clay wished there was something he could say to his father to ease the hopelessness, take away the grief that clung to his father like a shroud. But there was nothing short of returning his mother alive and well that would transform Thomas back into the man he had been.

It took him only a moment to go into the bedroom and pull the spread off the bed. He awkwardly folded it as best he could, and then carried it back into the living room beneath his arm.

"Thanks, Dad. I'll have it back to you in a day or so."

They murmured goodbyes, then Clay took Tamara by the elbow and pulled her out the front door, out of the house that oozed only the grief and despair of a man who'd lost his soul mate.

* * *

Tamara took the spread from Clay and held it in her lap as they pulled away from the ranch house. She ran her hand lightly over the slightly slick, blue-flowered material. "It must be so difficult for you to see your father that way…so beaten down and defeated."

"Yeah…it is hard. He's always been bigger than life, loud and passionate about everything and everyone. But without Mom he's become just a shell. And with each day that passes with no break in the case, he withdraws further and further into himself."

Again she stroked a hand over the bedspread. "Is this a new spread?" she asked.

He cast her a quick glance. "Not real new…maybe seven or eight months old. Why?"

"It doesn't feel like it's ever been washed."

"What do you mean?"

"It feels like it still has the sizing or whatever it is that they have when they haven't been washed," she explained.

"That's impossible," he said. "As recently as a week before she disappeared Mom washed the spread. In fact, she was mad because Dad had spilled grape juice on it and she didn't think she could get it out."

"I hate to be contrary, but I really don't believe this spread has been through a wash cycle."

"But that doesn't make sense," he protested.

"I'm just telling you what I think." She flashed him a quick smile. "You never told me I had to make sense."

"We'll know soon enough. As soon as we get home I intend to go over it with a magnifying glass and see if I can tell if there are any places where threads have been ripped."

"If you have two magnifying glasses, we can do it in half the time," she said.

This time his gaze lingered a moment longer on her. "Sometimes I think you just might be too good to be true."

She smiled. "Not at all. I just…I just want to help you." She stumbled over the words, appalled to realize she'd almost said she loved him.

She was grateful when they reached his house and they immediately got to work. They laid the bedspread flat on the living room floor, then each armed with a large magnifying glass, they began going over it inch by inch.

Tamara knew it was quite possible this was a waste of time, that the threads might not even be from the bedspread. But she had to admit the color looked right, as did the mix of polyester and cotton.

If they found a place where the threads had been torn, then the mystery of those threads Clay had found in the striker plate would be solved.

But they found no place where the threads on the bedspread had been ripped or torn. They traded places and went over it a second time and still found nothing.

"There doesn't seem to be any grape juice stain anywhere, either," Tamara said. She sat on her haunches at one end of the spread and Clay sat on the opposite end, a wrinkle of confusion cutting into his forehead.

"I don't understand it. You really think this hasn't been washed?"

"All I can tell you is that it's got the feel of a brand-new bedspread," she replied.

His gaze held hers from across the blue flowered

material. Dark and troubled, he stared at her, but it was obvious he was lost in deep concentration. "This isn't their spread."

"What do you mean? We just drove over and you took it from their bed."

"I know…" He raked a hand through his hair, his frown cutting deeper across his forehead. "When Mom first disappeared Alyssa kept getting visions of her in her bedroom. Alyssa said she knew it was Mom's bedroom because the bedspread was the same."

He ran his hand over the spread, lost in thought. Whatever he was thinking wasn't pleasant, for his eyes seemed to grow darker, more haunted by the moment.

She wanted to reach out to him, to take away the haunting that shadowed his eyes, but she knew nothing could…nothing except the return of his mother to the family…to the son who loved her.

"What are you thinking?" she finally asked, unable to stand it any longer.

He looked at her with eyes filled with torture. "What I'm thinking is that this isn't the bedspread that covered my parents' bed for the past eight or nine months. This spread was put on the bed the night that my mother disappeared."

"But why? Why would somebody do something like that?"

His fingers bunched up so that he held a fistful of the material. "I don't know the why, but if what I'm thinking is true, then this wasn't a crime of opportunity. This was thought out long in advance by somebody who knew my parents well, by somebody who had been in their house, seen the spread on their bed. This was done by somebody they trusted.''

Tamara gasped. It was bad enough to believe a stranger had entered their house, nearly killed Thomas and apparently kidnapped Rita. It was far worse to contemplate that such a thing had been done by a trusted friend or acquaintance. "What are you going to do now?" she asked as Clay rose from the floor.

"Call my sisters and see if they know where Mom might have bought the spread. If my theory is right, then somebody recently bought that same spread and I'm hoping the spread is the trail that leads to Mom."

As he got on the phone, Tamara scooted around so she could look at the tag to see the brand of the bedspread and if there was a particular name of the pattern.

By the time he'd hung up from speaking to both sisters, she had the information written on a sheet of paper for him. "Select Bedding is the brand and Blue Wisteria is the pattern."

"Thanks." He took the piece of paper from her. "Neither Breanna nor Savannah have a clue where she might have bought the spread."

She followed him into the kitchen where he pulled a phone book from the cabinet then sat at the table in the chair next to where she'd been sitting and sketching before he'd arrived home.

"What's next?" she asked, also sitting at the table.

"Mom was a firm believer in keeping Cherokee Corners money in Cherokee Corners. She would have bought the bedspread here in town." He opened the phone book to the yellow pages section. "It's probably too close to closing time for me to get any answers from anyone tonight, but I'll make a list of the stores that carry bedding, then start first thing in the morning and see what I can find out.''

''Do you want me to make some coffee?''

''That would be great.''

By the time the coffee was finished brewing he had a dozen names of stores written on a sheet of paper. He raked a hand through his hair and reared back in the chair. ''This is such a long shot,'' he said more to himself than to her. ''There are only three ways I'm going to find out who purchased a spread like Mom's. If the purchase was a charge, or a delivery, or if some salesclerk remembers who bought it.''

''Clay, you can't think negatively before you even begin the search,'' she said as she poured him a cup of coffee. She carried it over to where he sat and as he reached for it he bumped her sketch pad.

The pad flipped and landed faceup on the floor. ''Sorry,'' he said and reached down to grab the pad. He froze halfway to the floor and she knew he was looking at a sketch she'd never intended him to see. He picked the pad up and laid it on the table, sketch side up. ''What's this?''

''It's just a sketch,'' she said and reached out to turn the pad over. He grabbed her wrist to halt her, his gaze still focused on the sketch.

It had been strictly a labor of love. It was a picture of Clay, long, straight hair streaming over his shoulders. He was clad in a pair of tight jeans and a traditional Cherokee ribbon shirt.

When he looked at her, his eyes were filled with cool anger. ''You can sketch it, paint it or dream it, but I'm never going to be this man.'' He released her wrist.

''It…it doesn't mean anything,'' she said quickly.

She couldn't stand the sudden distance his eyes radiated as he gazed at her. "I was just messing around...I'm an artist...I sketch what's in my head. Clay...I'm in love with you."

She wasn't sure whether she spoke the words as some sort of crazy defense or simply because she couldn't hold them inside her heart for another minute.

Abruptly, he shoved away from the table and stood. The frown he'd worn before had only been a hint of the one that now tormented his features.

He thumped a finger against the sketch. "That's who you're in love with. Some Cherokee warrior who's only a figment of your imagination." He raked a hand through his hair, his gaze not quite meeting hers. "We've been foolish, playing house and making love when both of us know there's no future with each other."

The words, even though she'd thought them to herself before, spoken out loud by him devastated her. No future. She'd recognized it with her head, but her heart still refused to fully accept it.

She took a step toward where he stood, but he held up a hand to halt her, as if he couldn't stand the thought of her near him. "Clay...I love you, but I don't understand you. You are Cherokee, and no matter how much you deny it, that's who you are."

"I'm half Cherokee. My father is Irish."

"But, you are Cherokee nevertheless. Why have you turned your back on that part of you? Please, help me understand," she begged.

"I already told you what happened...what made me realize I didn't want to be Native anymore." His voice was curt, the words clipped.

She gazed at him in amazement. "You mean because a bunch of silly boys made fun of you years ago? That's it? That's all there is to it?"

His eyes flashed with anger. "You weren't there. You have no idea what I went through."

"You've allowed childhood pain to follow you into adulthood and dictate who you've become." A frustrated anger rose up inside her, an anger bred in the growing hopelessness that filled her heart.

"You've known from the beginning who I am and what I believe. Science…that's all that matters to me," he said.

"You hide in your science," she scoffed, surprised to feel the heat of tears coursing down her cheeks, tears bred in heartbreak. "Because you have nothing else in your life…because you've turned your back on the man you could be."

"You're the one who talks about how important it is to remember the nature of the beast," he retorted, "but somehow you forgot my nature."

"I didn't forget it, Clay." She swiped at her tears impatiently. She hadn't wanted him to see her cry. "I know that inside you is that warrior, proud and strong and stubborn, but he's been blanketed with so much baggage you've lost touch with him."

"I know who I am and I'm not that man." There was pain in his eyes as he held her gaze. "And I can't be the man to share the future you see for yourself."

She drew a tremulous breath, unable to staunch the tears that swam in her eyes. "You're right, Clay. The man I eventually marry will be proud of his roots. When we have children it will be as important to him that we take them to the cultural center, where they can share in the extended family that's there and learn wisdom from the elders by listening to their story-telling. I want my children to be proud of their Cherokee blood and the strength and grace of the Cherokee people.''

The pain she'd felt when she'd left Max had nothing on the wrenching heartache that tormented her now. She'd never really believed Max had loved her for anything other than her talent as an artist. But, Clay…she knew when she gazed into his eyes that he loved her, not as an artist, but as a woman.

''You know the really sad part about all this? I believe you love me as much as you're capable of loving, but even if you wanted a future with me, it wouldn't be enough.'' His eyes narrowed, but he remained silent and she continued. ''As long as you hate who you are, you'll never be able to truly love anyone else.''

With these final words she turned and ran. He didn't try to stop her and she knew it was because there was nothing more to say.

She ran into the bedroom where she'd been staying, half-blinded by the tears that seemed to be burning hotter, flowing like a river down her cheeks.

He was right about one thing. They had both been fools, sleeping together, eating together, spending quiet time in the evenings together. They had been indulging in a pretend marriage of sorts.

The only thing she was left with was a very real broken heart.

When Rita thought of her husband, she couldn't stand the pain. Even if she managed to escape from this prison, or was found and rescued, what would her life be like without her Thomas?

From the moment she'd met him when he'd been a handsome police officer, she'd known he was the man for her, the man who would father her children and share her dreams.

That momentary glimpse she'd gotten of him before she'd been drugged and carried from their home had devastated her. There had been too much blood and he'd been too still to think anything but the worst.

And her poor children, not only coping with her disappearance, but also with their father's death. Her heart embraced them all…. Breanna, who had been so wounded when the man who fathered little Maggie had left her. Savannah, who had lost her husband in a tragic car accident. And Clay.

She lay on the bed on the familiar bedspread and thought of her eldest son. She'd had little else to do but think while in this place and with thinking came regrets.

She needed to tell her son some things, share with him some insight she'd gained. She hoped she got the opportunity.

A clang of metal resounded and then the wide slit in the metal door opened, revealing another box like the one she had previously received.

Scattered on the floor around her bed were the pieces of the first dress that had come in such a box. The dress had terrified her, as if whoever held her captive wanted to dress her up like a doll.

This box terrified her, too. Did it hold another dress, or something to punish her for ripping up the last one? Should she open it or leave it be?

She dragged a hand across her chest, trying to still the frantic beating of her heart. What worried her most was the fact that she knew she was in the middle of some sort of psychological game. She was terrified that eventually, if she was found and rescued, it would be too late…she'd already be stark, raving mad.

Chapter 15

The words they had exchanged the night before had been inevitable, Clay thought as he sat at his desk the next morning. It was too early to begin calling stores to find out about the bedspread and too late to stop the flood of emotions that had spewed out of Tamara last night.

He could have stopped it. He could have stopped it at any time from the moment he'd met her. He'd allowed his attraction for her to blind him to the truth—that they were headed for disaster.

He should have never allowed her to move in with him, and he sure as hell should have never made love to her. Even now, the thought of her warm, willing body in his arms stirred him and at the same time the memory of her tears pained him.

"You're in unusually early."

Clay looked up to see Glen Cleberg standing in his

doorway. Clay rose to his feet, not returning the smile that the chief offered him.

"Tell me something, Chief, knowing that I was hunting down people who had landscaped with Dalmatian rock in my parents' case, why in the hell didn't you tell me you've got that rock at your house?"

Glen frowned. "I thought I did tell you."

"No, no you didn't." Clay heard the sharpness in his tone.

"Clay, I've got a serial killer stabbing the young men of this town. I thought I told you, if I didn't, then I apologize. I've had a lot on my mind."

"It's kind of a big thing to forget to tell me."

Chief Cleberg eyed him curiously. "You think I had something to do with what happened to your parents, Clay? I'll admit your father and I haven't always seen things eye-to-eye, but I like arguing with the stubborn old man. Half my energy is spent trying to best the records of old Chief Thomas James. And as far as your mother…I've got a wife and three single daughters. Why in the hell would I want another woman in my house?"

It was the longest impromptu speech Clay had ever heard Glen speak. "I'm sorry if I sounded accusatory," he said.

Glen's gaze was sympathetic. "I know how tough this has been on you, Clay. But we ran into a dead end with your parents' case long ago."

"I might have something new… It's too soon to tell if it's going to be important or not," Clay said.

"You know if anything comes up, we'll move heaven and earth to get your mother back to you," Glen said.

"I know that. I'll keep you posted if anything breaks."

A moment later Clay was once again alone in the lab. He returned to his desk and back to thoughts of Tamara.

She was the first woman he'd ever spent any time with that had made him wish for more, made him believe that marriage and children would have been nice…if he'd been a different kind of man…if she'd been a different kind of woman.

He rubbed his forehead where a headache threatened to take hold. He'd slept little the night before. What he'd wanted to do was go into her room, take her into his arms and kiss away the tears that had washed down her face. What he'd wanted to do was take her into his bedroom, hold her in his arms through the night and wish the night would last forever.

Enough, he commanded himself. He had plenty to do besides sit at his desk and pine for a woman who would never, could never be his.

He quickly made phone calls to both his sisters and gave them each four stores to check for the bedspread. He didn't tell them what he needed the information for, only that he needed to know who might have bought a spread like the one that their mother had owned.

He'd kept five stores for him to check out himself and the minute ten o'clock arrived and he knew the stores were open, he began his calls.

He was interrupted off and on, but by noon he'd made all the calls and had come up empty. None of the stores on his list carried the Select Bedding brand.

The nature of the beast. He wasn't sure why but

that catch phrase haunted him. What nature of beast hit a man over the head then stole his woman? What nature of beast took a mother away from her family? He had no idea what the answer was, but felt it was important that he discover it.

By noon Savannah had checked in. Her investigation of the stores on her list had yielded the same result as Clay had with his list. Nothing.

Bitterly disappointed, Clay waited for Breanna to check in. Last night when he and Tamara had made the startling realization that the spread they were examining was not the spread that had been on Rita's bed before the crime, for the first time in weeks hope had welled up inside Clay.

Maybe they'd get lucky, maybe this was the key that would unlock the mystery, and maybe there really was a chance that they'd get his mother home safe and sound and where she belonged.

But with each minute that ticked by, that hope was growing harder and harder to sustain. As that hope seeped away, the pain of Tamara seemed to grow substantially.

Along with the heartache of Tamara was the responsibility to find whomever it was that had tormented her with her legend. All the students, both young and old, had been questioned concerning the vandalism both at the school and at her cottage. The few that had not been able to provide an alibi for the afternoon of the attack on the cottage were unlikely suspects to begin with.

He'd never felt so impotent…so inadequate. He couldn't find his mother. He couldn't finger a serial killer. He couldn't find a vandal. And he couldn't be the man who Tamara would spend her life with.

You've brought childhood hurts into adulthood and allowed them to dictate the man you've become. That's what she had told him and he refused to consider if there might be any validity to her words. It didn't matter.

It was almost three when Breanna came into the lab, her pretty features taut with tension. "I hit pay dirt," she said without preamble. "Evans." The name was of an upscale local store that specialized in home furnishing. "They had the brand and the name and it just so happened that particular pattern, Blue Wisteria, was sold three months ago. He paid cash for it."

"He?" Clay jumped up from his desk. "How do you know it was a he?"

"The saleslady specifically remembered the sale. She told me the gentleman knew just what he was looking for and had told her that wisteria was one of his favorite flowers."

"Did she get a name?" Clay felt his pulse pound at his temples. "Did she know the man who bought it?"

Breanna stared at him in bewilderment. "Clay, what's this all about?"

"Just tell me who it is, Breanna, that's all I need to know."

"Jacob Kincaid."

Clay stared at her as if she'd just spoken some strange foreign language. "What?" He needed her to repeat it, to make certain he'd heard what he'd thought he'd heard.

"Three months ago Jacob Kincaid went into Evans and bought a Select Bedding bedspread in the pattern of Blue Wisteria. I guess he saw Mom and Dad's spread and liked it."

Of course, it was impossible for Breanna to see anything evil. After all, they were talking about Jacob Kincaid, respected banker and best friend of the family. But Clay's blood ran cold at the implications.

"Go home, Breanna. Go home and stay by the phone."

"Tell me what's going on, Clay."

He placed a hand on her shoulder. "I'll tell you what's going on as soon as I know."

"But surely you don't think Jacob had anything to do with what happened to Mom and Dad? He's our friend, Clay. He even put up a reward to help find Mom."

"I know, Bree. I'm just trying to figure some things out. I'll let you know what's up when I have all the information I need."

Minutes later, after Breanna had left, Clay got into his car and headed toward the Kincaid mansion. He knew Jacob would be at work. He also knew that he could do nothing to compromise the integrity of the scene...if there was a scene.

At the moment all he had was a bedspread bought a month before the crime had occurred...hardly a crime in and of itself. What he needed was something more...something to take to Glen that would galvanize the entire force.

There was a huge part of Clay that found it almost impossible to consider that Jacob could have anything to do with his mother's disappearance. Clay had been in Jacob's house, had sat in the kitchen and drank coffee since Rita had disappeared.

He clenched his fingers around the steering wheel. Yes, it was almost impossible to believe that Jacob would have anything to do with all this...almost.

Tamara's legend came back to haunt him. The nature of the beast. A man stays true to his nature. And what was Jacob's nature? Clay had always believed it to be one of benevolence, a kind man who liked nice things. A lonely man who loved his collection of fine items.

Was it possible at some time in his life Jacob had been collecting women? The thought made a hot anger and an icy chill race in Clay's veins.

There was no car parked in front of the three-story mansion. Clay got out of the car, for the first time looking at the place with the eyes of a cop instead of the eyes of a friend.

There were lots of rooms in the house Clay had never been invited into. What secrets might those rooms hold? Did one of them hold his mother?

It took all the willpower he possessed not to storm the front door, break it down and rush inside. If he did that and he was wrong, then he'd wind up jobless and probably behind bars. If he did that and he was right, then any evidence that was found in the house would be thrown out and no matter what Jacob had done, he'd skate on a technicality.

He walked around the perimeter of the house, looking for something, anything that might yield a search warrant. It was just a feeling…a gut feeling, but he sensed his mother's presence. He knew in his gut that she was in the house.

He found what he was looking for at the back of the house. French doors led to a large patio area complete with brick barbecue grill. But that wasn't the only door at the back of the house. A small door led from what Clay assumed might be a mudroom and directly in front of that door in a semicircle pattern was Dalmatian rock blend.

Guilty. The word screamed through Clay's head. Two clues and both of them pointed directly to Jacob Kincaid. With his heart racing, he ran back to his car and headed back to the station.

"What's going on here?" Jacob demanded as he got out of his car and stared at the police officers that were awaiting his arrival. "I was in the middle of an important meeting at the bank when Chief Cleberg called and told me to get home." His gaze landed on Clay. "Clay, would you please tell me what's going on?"

Bitter betrayal coursed through Clay as he looked at the man he'd considered a favorite uncle, a confidante, and a friend. He held out the folded paperwork that Glen had obtained for him only fifteen minutes before. "This is a search warrant, Jacob. We figured we'd extend you the courtesy of being here while we execute it."

"A search warrant?" Jacob frowned. "But why? What on earth are you looking for? Clay, I'm sure this is all just a terrible misunderstanding. Tell me exactly what you want and we'll get this straightened out before you have your men traipsing all through my house."

A bead of sweat worked its way down Jacob's face. It could have been the punishing four o'clock heat or it could be a sign of guilt. In any case, it galvanized Clay into action. "It's all in the warrant," he said curtly. "You want to unlock the door for us or would you prefer we bust it down?"

Jacob gasped, apparently thinking of his ornate

front door splintered by force. He fumbled in his pocket and pulled out a ring of keys. "I don't understand this. This is a huge mistake," he muttered as he unlocked the door. He opened the door then stepped back to allow the officers inside.

"Sheller, Malcolm and Bailey, you take this floor. Rogers, Creighton and Stanley, you take the second floor. I'll take the third," Clay said. "Zeller, you stay here with Mr. Kincaid, see to it that he doesn't go anyplace."

As the men began to move, Clay looked at Jacob once again. "I hope I'm wrong, Jacob. I really hope I'm wrong." Jacob didn't reply.

Heart pounding, adrenaline rushing, Clay turned to make his way to the stairs. As he passed the glass display cabinets that held all the things Jacob had collected over the years, his mind raced with possibilities.

Jacob had told him he'd never married because he'd never found the perfect woman. Had he been collecting women until he found the perfect one, disposing of the ones who had not been deemed flawless?

Were they already too late? Had he already disposed of his mother? Grief ripped at him at the very thought. Savannah and Riley believed that the person who had kidnapped his mother had held her for at least six months before killing her. He prayed that for his mother it wasn't too late.

He'd never been to the third floor of the mansion. Jacob had shown him around the second floor where there were several guest bedrooms a long time ago, but he'd never invited Clay to view the top floor.

A narrow staircase led from second to third floor

and as he climbed it Clay's heart felt as if it might pound right out of his chest.

When he reached the landing he looked down the long hallway. There were three closed doors on the left and three closed doors on the right. He touched the butt of his gun in his holster. He was certain he wouldn't need the gun, but it was comforting to know it was within quick reach.

He went to the first door on the left and opened it. Inside was a room filled with African artwork. A body-size wooden crate lay in the middle of the room and as Clay approached it he breathed shallowly from his mouth, his nerves taut with tension.

Nails held the top of the crate in place. What was inside? What if he pulled the top off and found his mother's body stuffed inside? He spied a hammer nearby and picked it up. His hands shook as he walked over to the crate.

In the distance from the downstairs area he could hear other officers talking to one another, but the buzzing in his ears muted their voices. Using the back of the hammer, he pried out the first nail, then a second.

Within seconds he had all the nails out and only had to lift the top of the crate to see what was inside. He sent a silent prayer upward to the Creator of all, then slid the top of the crate off the box. Air whooshed out of him in relief. Inside was a mask made of wood about six feet long.

He left the room, his legs feeling slightly shaky and went into the next one. It was obviously a storage area filled with cast-off furniture.

He checked two rooms on the right and found

much the same things…old furniture, stacks of newspapers, file cabinets and miscellaneous.

There were only two rooms left and he had a sinking feeling in the pit of his stomach. What if he'd been wrong? What if Jacob had truly bought the bedspread because he'd seen his parents' and had loved the pattern? What if all this was for nothing?

He couldn't think about that now. He went to the last door on the left side of the hall and tried to turn the knob, then spied the padlock that kept the door from opening. Once again adrenaline ripped through him. Why would somebody lock a door on the third floor of a home if not to hide something? Or keep somebody inside?

He knocked on the door. "Hello? Anyone in there? Mom? Are you there?" Pressing his ear against the wood, he listened intently. Nothing. No sound escaped.

He raced down both flights of stairs. Jason Sheller met him on the bottom floor. "We're all clear here," he said.

"I've got a padlocked door up on the third floor," Clay said. "Either Kincaid gives us the key or we go through the door."

He found Jacob on the front porch with Chief Cleberg. Clay approached them, fighting the need to wrap his hands around Jacob Kincaid's stout neck. "Where's the key, Jacob?"

The man blinked once, then twice more. "What key?"

"Don't play games with me," Clay said and took a menacing step forward.

"I'll unlock the door," Jacob said.

Clay followed him back up the stairs. Neither of

them spoke a word until they reached the second landing. "Where did you get the rock that's all around your back door?"

"What?" Jacob appeared bewildered by the question.

"The black and white speckled rock. Where did you get it? We've checked landscaping services and quarries and you aren't on any of the lists as a buyer."

"What does this have to do with anything? I'm an important man. Why are you doing this to me, Clay?" he said impatiently.

"Just answer the question."

"How dare you treat me like this," Jacob continued to bluster. "You've been a guest in my home. You've always been welcome here. We were friends."

"Where did you get the gravel, Jacob?" Clay wasn't about to be moved by the man's words.

Jacob sighed impatiently. "A neighbor ordered some. He had more than he could use and offered me a couple of wheelbarrows of the rock. Is that a crime?"

Clay didn't answer, but instead gestured toward the locked door. "Unlock it."

"Whatever you're looking for, you aren't going to find it here. This is just a small room that holds my security cameras and equipment." He unlocked the door and shoved it open. "See?"

Clay wondered how many times a heart could be filled with hope only to have those hopes shattered. The room was exactly what Jacob had said it was. A small room, it held a console of monitors, all dark and apparently turned off. A large luxurious office chair sat before the console and there was nothing else in the room.

"I told you there was nothing in here," Jacob said, a note of triumph in his deep voice. "Now, take your men and get the hell out of my house."

He'd been so sure. It had all fit so neatly...the presence of the Dalmatian rock, the purchase of the bedspread, the nature of the man...Clay had been so certain that Jacob Kincaid had his mother.

"Clay, I can forgive all this. I know you've been under a tremendous amount of pressure and stress." Jacob reached out to close the door.

Clay slapped the door with his arm to halt Jacob pulling it closed, his mind whirling. Who put a bank of cameras in an upstairs room and kept it locked? And if these were really security cameras, who sat and monitored them?

"What are you doing?" Jacob asked as Clay approached the console.

"Just checking out your security system." Clay saw the power switch and reached for it.

"Clay...It works fine," Jacob said frantically.

Clay flipped the power switch and the monitors came to life. His breath caught in his throat. He was looking at what appeared to be his mother's bedroom. The bed looked the same, the spread the same, even the nightstand and the Tiffany-style mission lamp were exactly the same. On the bed was his mother...as still as a corpse, her eyes closed.

Clay turned to Jacob and with a roar of rage he hit the older man in the shoulders and backed him up against the hall. "Where is she?" he cried. "Where in the hell do you have her?" He moved his hands from Jacob's beefy shoulders to his neck and squeezed. "Tell me where she is, you sick bastard."

Jacob coughed, his face turning a florid color as Clay squeezed tighter and tighter. "In the basement," he managed to choke out. "There's a book-case…behind it."

Clay released him and he slumped down to the floor, coughing uncontrollably. He dug into his pocket and handed Clay his set of keys at the same time a handful of officers reached the top of the stairs and joined them.

"Sheller…cuff him." Clay didn't wait around to watch the task performed, instead he raced down the stairs to the bottom level where Glen stood, his face filled with anxiety.

"She's in the basement," Clay said and Glen followed him as he located the stairs that led down to the subterranean level.

When they hit the basement, it took a moment for Clay to orient himself. He located a light switch to illuminate the utter darkness and found himself standing in a rec room.

It was a room within a room, but the interior room was made of soundproof material and had a metal door.

"Clay." Glen placed his hand on Clay's arm before he could get the key into the locked metal door. "Before you open this you need to prepare yourself. We don't know what kind of condition she might be in."

Clay nodded impatiently. All he knew was that on the other side of the door was his mother. He unlocked the door and swung it open.

His mother was still stretched out on the bed, her

eyes closed, her beautiful features without any animation. For a split second, a sweeping pain threatened to tumble him to his knees. Were they too late?

"E-'tsi." Mother, he whispered, unaware that he had spoken in Cherokee.

"I'm dreaming," she said, not opening her eyes.

"No dream. I've come to take you home." He rushed to the side of the bed and Rita opened her eyes and cried out. "Clay…my son. I knew you'd come." She got up from the bed and threw herself into his arms. Glen remained in the doorway, silent and respectful of the mother/son reunion.

Clay clung to his mother as a dam of emotions broke loose and he wept. His mother cried as well, clinging to him as if she'd never let him go.

Later, as he led her from Jacob Kincaid's home and to his patrol car, she walked proudly and without help beside him. "I can't believe it was Jacob," she said.

"From what Glen told me he's making a full confession. Apparently you were the third woman he'd taken. He killed the other two."

"Then he would have eventually killed me as well, for I would have never become whatever it was he wanted." She got into the passenger side of the car and waited until he'd slid behind the wheel.

"Do you need to go to the hospital, Mom? Glen said you should be checked out."

She shook her head vehemently. "I was not physically harmed and all I want to do is see my family."

"There's been some changes, Mom," he warned her. After all, she had no idea that Breanna had gotten married and was pregnant and that Savannah was engaged.

"I know." Rita was silent for a long moment and

Clay wondered what kind of trauma she would have to overcome. He reached out and touched her hand. "You'll be fine, Mom. We'll all be fine."

They traveled for a few minutes in silence, then Rita spoke again. "I was in that room day after day and had nothing to do but think and there are some things I need to say to you, my son."

She gestured for him to pull over to the side of the road. "I want your full attention and I can't wait another minute to speak the thoughts that have burdened my heart."

He pulled over, cut the engine, then turned to face her curiously. She was so beautiful with her jet-black hair, dark eyes and proud features. The few lines that lived on her face had come from smiles, lines that wrinkled the corners of her eyes and proved that there had been far more laughter than tears in her lifetime.

"Clay." She reached out and took his hand in hers. "We said some terrible things to each other the day before all this happened."

Guilt rocketed through him and he squeezed her hand tightly. "Mom...I..."

She shook her head to still the apology before it could leave his lips. "You were my firstborn and I fell in love with you the moment I looked at your face...so strong and so beautiful. You were my little *a-ya-wis-gi*, my warrior, and I raised you as such."

She frowned. "But there were too many times when I was too much Cherokee and not enough mother to you. I was so busy celebrating our heritage, building the cultural center that I didn't listen enough to you and the turmoil my work and the world were wreaking in your life."

"Mom, that was a long time ago," he protested.

''Perhaps,'' she agreed. Her eyes were filled with such love for him he felt it inside him. ''But sometimes childhood scars don't heal, they fester and make the soul sick. If you needed more of me than you got, then I'm sorry.''

Her eyes filled with tears and Clay felt the burn of his own tears. ''I won't ever again ask you to participate in the cultural center events. I'll accept that this is not the path you chose and I'll respect that.''

Her words made something break loose inside Clay, a hardness that had encased his heart began to shatter. Had he needed more of his mother in those years when he'd been teased and tormented for being Cherokee? Perhaps. But years had passed, the town was different and suddenly he wasn't sure what path he wanted to walk for the rest of his life.

''I love you, Mom.'' He squeezed her hand gently, then released it and started the engine. ''And if I don't get you back to the ranch house immediately, Dad's going to skin me alive.''

Rita gasped and clutched his arm. ''Dad? Your father…he's alive?'' Deep sobs ripped through her. ''I thought he was dead…all I remember was seeing him on the floor and all the blood…I thought he was dead.''

''He's alive, Mom. I thought you knew. But since you've been gone he's only been half-alive. He's still rehabilitating from the blow he took to the head, but I have a feeling the moment he sees you, he's going to have a miraculous recovery.''

''Hurry, Clay. I need my Thomas,'' she cried. Clay pushed the button that made a siren blare and pressed the gas pedal to the floor.

Within minutes they pulled up in front of the house

where he recognized both his sisters' cars in the driveway. But there was only a single person standing on the porch—Thomas—and he looked more handsome and stronger than Clay had seen him since the crime had occurred.

Before Clay had brought the car to a full halt, Rita was out of the passenger door and racing for the porch. Thomas met her halfway. Tears of joy welled up Clay's eyes as he watched his mother and father embrace.

There would be much joy in the James home tonight, but Clay wouldn't be there to share in it. He wanted to talk to Tamara, needed to tell her that with her help Rita was back home safe and sound where she belonged.

He honked, waved, then turned the car around and headed toward his own house.

He knew the moment he entered the house that she was no longer there. The scent of her still lingered, but the energy she'd brought with her had disappeared.

He made a fast phone call to the station and learned that Jacob was not only confessing to hitting his father and kidnapping his mother, but he'd also confessed to two more similar crimes.

In those two cases, the men had been killed and eventually so had the women. One of those cases was Riley Frazier's parents. At least his future brother-in-law would have final closure.

He was on his way out of the house when he saw the two pieces of the courting flute that had belonged to Tamara still on the bookcases behind his worktable. She must have forgotten them. He took the pieces with him and headed for her cottage.

She'd been with him through his foul moods and despair, it seemed only right that she know that his mother was home safe.

Chapter 16

Home. She was home again…and alone.

Tamara had awakened early that morning knowing that she couldn't spend another night in Clay's house. She heard him leave early, had waited until the house was once again silent, then had gotten out of bed and packed to leave.

The heartache of loving Clay was almost too great to bear and she had known that to spend one more minute, one more hour, one more night in his home was impossible.

By ten she'd been packed and had called a cab to bring her back here. The cabby had dropped her off and she was relieved to see that all the windows had been replaced and at least from the outside the place didn't look any worse for the wear.

She approached the front door, steeling herself for what kind of a mess still might be inside. When she unlocked and opened the front door, she breathed a sigh of relief.

Jeb had done well. The floor was swept clean of all breakage. The deep rents in the sofa had been repaired with upholstery thread and needle. Although the shelves that had once held her hummingbird collection were now bare, she knew that eventually she would be able to fill them again…just as eventually her heart would mend.

The one thing she'd needed to do was keep busy. She had to find something, anything to do to keep her mind off Clay. Painting was out of the question. Her heart ached too deeply to feel creative.

She spent the next several hours absorbed in the task of trying to glue back together some of the hummingbird figurines that had meant so much to her.

As she worked, thoughts and memories of Clay continued to intrude, but she resolutely shoved them away. She and Clay had indulged in a kind of fantasy for a while, but now the fantasy was over and it was time to get back to her real life.

She had students to teach, paintings to paint and a cottage to put back together again. She had no place in her life for a man like Clay.

Apparently he had no place for her in his life as well. Somewhere in the back of her mind, she'd been expecting…hoping for a phone call from him. Surely he must know she was gone by now, but her phone remained silent.

By five that evening, tired of gluing bits and pieces back together, heartsick and lonely, she stretched out on her sofa and looked at the sketches she had done while at Clay's house.

The one he had seen of himself hadn't been the

only one she'd drawn of him. There was a sketch of him at his worktable, one of him asleep and the one of him as a warrior that had caused their fight.

Each and every sketch caused a rip through her heart. She jumped as the phone rang. When she answered it was Alyssa. "I just heard yesterday that you'd been staying at Clay's," she said. "I tried there this morning then decided to try you here."

"Yeah, I'm just getting settled back in."

"Are you sure that's wise? I mean, they still don't know who trashed your house."

"I'll be fine here. I have good locks on the doors. Besides, I couldn't stay at Clay's any longer."

"I don't know, Tamara, I'm worried about you." Alyssa hesitated a moment, then continued, "I had a vision of you, Tamara, you and a monster. In my vision, the monster ripped out your heart."

A half sob, half burst of laughter escaped Tamara. "That wasn't a monster, that was your cousin, Clay."

There was a long moment of silence. "Oh, Tamara, I'm sorry," Alyssa finally said.

"Just please, whatever you do, don't say I told you so," Tamara replied, wiping at the tears that had come unbidden from her eyes.

"I'd never do that. Is there anything I can do?"

"No. I'll just lick my wounds for a few days, concentrate on some painting and I'll be fine."

"Want to meet for lunch tomorrow?"

"No, thanks. I appreciate the invite, but I'd like to spend a couple of days here getting settled back in."

"You'll call me?"

Tamara smiled. "You know I will." They said goodbye then Tamara hung up the phone. She curled back up on the sofa, noting that outside the window the sun was beginning to set.

"Gv-ge-yu-hi." I love you. She whispered the words aloud, Clay's face a mental picture in her head. She closed her eyes against the tears that once again threatened to fall. How many tears could she shed over one man? A heartful...and that was plenty.

She hadn't realized she'd fallen asleep until she awakened to the sounds of footsteps once again clattering on her porch. She wasn't sure what time it was, but she knew in her heart it could only be Clay.

She jumped up off the sofa, raced to the door and pulled it open. A monster rushed in, shoving her backward, then standing in the doorway and growling ominously.

The bear. The bear from the legend come alive. Although someplace in the back of Tamara's head she knew that beneath the bear fur and skull there was a human being. But at the moment rational thought was vanquished beneath shock and fear.

As the bear roared, claws scratched high in the air...claws that appeared to be razor sharp. "I have come for you my Native princess," he said.

It was only when she heard his voice that she recognized who was beneath the bearskin. Terry Black. Certainly identifying him did nothing to alleviate her fear.

Terry was a big, tall, burly eighteen-year-old. She knew he had a reputation as a bully, that he enjoyed hurting people.

"I'm not a Native princess, Terry," she said, trying to keep the terror out of her voice as she backed away from him.

He stepped into the door and closed it behind him.

"I've been waiting out there in the woods…night after night…waiting for you to come back here."

"Go home, Terry. Go home before you do something you'll regret." At the same time she spoke these words, her gaze darted around the room, frantically seeking a weapon of some kind.

"I'm not going anywhere until my job here is done." Terry pulled off the bear skull so she could clearly see his dark eyes…eyes that glittered with the anticipation of evil.

"Everyone's been shaking in their boots about the slasher serial killer, but after tonight, they will fear the power and destruction of the bear."

With these words, he advanced toward her.

Was it only last night that he and Tamara had fought? It seemed like a lifetime ago, Clay thought as he drove to her cottage. The day had been so full. And now his mother was home safe and sound and the wounds that had been inflicted on his family would be healed.

And those moments in the car alone with his mother had also healed some old wounds and created a confusion inside him. He shoved those thoughts aside. He just wanted to see Tamara now and let her know his mother was home safe.

When he pulled up in front of the cottage, he knew instantly that something was wrong. Although the front door was closed, silhouetted against the front window were two figures, not one.

One of those figures appeared huge, the other one much smaller and although it appeared they were moving in a strange dance of sorts, he knew it wasn't a dance. It was a struggle.

Drawing his gun, he left the car and approached the house in a crouch, hoping the steadily falling night would obscure his movements.

He needed to see exactly what was going on before he acted. He crept up to the front porch and peered into the window. The scene that met his gaze froze his breath.

Tamara was backed up against the far wall of the living room, wielding a small lamp like a weapon against the big bearskin-clad man who attacked her. Blood poured from a wound in her cheek and as he watched the man slapped at her with a huge bear claw.

Clay wasted no time. He burst through the front door, but tripped over a sofa cushion that had somehow landed in front of the door. He flew forward and the gun left his hand, sliding into the shadows beneath the sofa.

He was up and on his feet in a second. The bear creature turned and Clay saw the face of a teenager. The boy's features were rather coarse, the glint in his eyes cunning and the twisted smile was filled with malevolence.

"Clay!" Tamara exclaimed, her voice filled with the terror that darkened her eyes.

"Well, well. What have we here? Another victim of the bear. The bear can take care of two of you." The young man roared as he waved the deadly claws in the air. "And people will talk about the bear's power for years to come."

"Nobody is going to talk about a dumb teenager dressed up for Halloween," Clay scoffed. He needed to draw the boy away from Tamara.

"You shut up. I'm not a dumb teenager," he exclaimed.

"It's Terry Black, Clay," Tamara said.

Terry growled and swiped one of those claws in her direction, just barely missing her other cheek. "You shut up, bitch."

"I thought in the legend the bear loves the Native princess," Clay said, advancing two steps closer.

"He kills her anyway," Terry replied. "And you'd better stop right there or I'll take her head off right now."

Clay stopped in his tracks, cursing the fact that he didn't have his gun, respecting the sharpness of those claws and desperate to get Terry away from Tamara.

"You're the one who vandalized the classroom," he said, buying time so he could figure out what to do. "And you destroyed the cottage last week."

Terry grinned. "I wanted people to know my power."

"But your mother gave you an alibi. She said you were cleaning out the garage on the day this place was wrecked."

Terry's grin fell. "That stupid cow does what I tell her to do. She knows better than to cross me."

"So, you beat up on your mother and then you come to attack a young woman who lives alone." Clay snorted in derision. "Typical bully behavior…terrorizing the weak but scared to face an equal threat. Face it, Terry. You aren't anything but a big bully and everyone knows that at heart bullies are cowards."

His words had the desired affect. With an enraged bellow, Terry charged him. The two men fell to the floor, Clay grappling to grip the claws that posed the most danger. "Run, Tamara," he yelled as he fought. "Go on, get out of here."

He felt a searing pain down his side, along with the ripping sound of his shirt and knew a claw had made contact with his chest. He managed to grab one claw, vaguely surprised to realize Terry had strapped the claws onto his arms and hands.

They rolled over and over again on the floor, Clay ending up on top of Terry, but the boy kept an arm free, swiping dangerously close to Clay's face. Clay finally managed to grab Terry's flailing hand. He held both the young man's wrists tight as Terry bucked and kicked to get free. The kid was strong, stout, but Clay was older, more experienced and determined that Terry Black would do no future harm.

"Do you need my help?"

Clay looked behind him to see her standing with the gun in her hand. It was pointed at Terry and she held it calmly, steadily.

Clay scrambled up and took the gun from her. "Go find some rope and a pair of scissors," he said. Tamara raced for the kitchen. "And you, don't move," he said to Terry.

"It was just a joke," Terry exclaimed and forced a laugh. "Come on, man. It was just a big joke. I didn't mean anything by it."

Clay touched his chest where blood oozed from where the claw had made contact. "When you draw blood, it's no joke."

Tamara returned with the items Clay had requested. He handed her the gun once again. "If he moves... shoot him."

"It would be my pleasure," she replied.

Armed with the scissors and rope, Clay first cut the

bear claws from Terry's arms and threw them across the room. He then tied the boy's hands behind his back and tied his feet together.

"That should hold him. I'll just call in and get somebody here to take him away." Clay made the call, then he and Tamara stood, watching Terry as they waited for his transport to jail.

"You son-of-a-bitch. You really think I'm going to jail? I'm going to come back for you," Terry yelled.

"Shut up before you irritate me," Clay warned.

Terry growled. "I'm the bear! I will have the Native princess."

Clay walked over to him and slammed his fist into Terry's mouth. Tamara gasped and Terry cried out as his bottom lip split and spurted blood. "I warned you," Clay said. "Native warriors don't like bears talking about their Native princesses."

Within minutes a squad car had arrived. Jason Sheller and his partner Charlie Zeller walked in. "What have we got here?" He looked at Terry, then looked at Clay and Tamara. "You two okay?"

"Fine. Just get this piece of varmint out of here. Book him for vandalism, criminal mischief and attempted murder. Tamara and I will be down at the station later to make a full statement."

The minute the officers and Terry were gone, Clay looked at Tamara. "I told you to run."

"I wasn't about to run and leave you here with him." She stepped closer to him and touched his chest. "We need to get this cleaned up," she said.

"And this…" He touched her cheek, grateful to see that it had finally stopped bleeding and the wound didn't look too deep.

"I've got some peroxide. Why don't you go into the kitchen and I'll be right in."

Clay nodded. Now that the drama was over, he could tell her about them finding his mother. Then he'd be on his way and that would be the end of their story.

As Tamara got the peroxide and cotton balls from the bathroom cabinet, she tried not to think of that moment when Clay had told Terry that a Native warrior didn't allow anyone to talk about a Native princess. Considering the man he professed to be, the words had seemed incongruent.

She took a moment and cleaned her cheek, pleased to see that the blow had been a glancing one and the wound was little more than a scratch.

Now that she had a moment to think, she wondered why Clay had come when he had. Certainly she'd wished and hoped that he'd come here and tell her he'd realized he couldn't live without her. But she knew that was just the fantasy of a broken heart.

She returned to the kitchen where he sat at her small table. He'd already taken off his torn shirt and she tried to steel herself against the sight of his beautiful chest, now sporting a long, bloody wound.

"It's not as bad as it looks," he assured her.

"It looks terrible." She dropped to her knees before him and began to swipe off the blood.

"Tamara, we found my mom."

Her gaze flew from his chest to his face. "What?"

The joy of his words shone from his eyes. "We found her alive and well and being held in Jacob Kincaid's basement."

"Oh, Clay!" Unmindful of the blood on his chest,

she reached up and hugged him, tears of happiness splashing on her cheeks.

She released him and got back to work. It had been too heady for that moment, being in his arms.

As she began cleaning the wound again, he explained to her about finding his mother and Kincaid's confession. "You helped so much, Tamara," he said when she'd finished cleaning him up.

"Me? How did I help?" She recapped the bottle of peroxide, then remained standing near the table.

"The nature of the beast. That's what made me sure Mom was in Kincaid's house. He was a collector. It was in his nature to covet things. It wasn't a big leap to realize he also might covet beautiful women."

He stood. "And that same philosophy held true with Terry Black. We should have looked at him more closely. It was in his nature to enjoy bullying…creating terror."

"I think something about the serial murders set him off," she said. "He was jealous that those murders were getting so much attention." It was so hard, to stand there and not want him. It wasn't just a physical want…it was the need to love him, to be loved by him, the need to have his children and build a life. A stupid, foolish need that would never come to pass.

"Thank you, Clay," she said and headed into the living room. As much as she needed him to stay, she wanted him to go. "He would have killed me if you hadn't shown up when you did."

He'd followed her into the living room, but instead of heading for the front door he sat on the sofa. "When I peeked into the window and saw you backed against the wall by him I swear my heart stopped.'' He patted the sofa next to him. "Sit with me.''

She hesitated a moment. She sank onto the sofa, keeping as much distance as possible between them.

He frowned and rubbed a hand across his forehead, then looked at her for a long moment without speaking. "Long ago I chose the path that I intended to walk,'' he finally said. "And until I met you I thought I was happy with the choices I'd made. You were right about one thing. I have taken childhood pains and carried them into my adult life, allowed them to dictate the choices I made.''

He broke eye contact with her and instead stared down at the coffee table in front of him. "When I was driving my mother back home, she had a talk with me.'' He looked back at her again. "Remember when I told you that I'd always felt as if the cultural center was another sibling?''

She nodded, unsure where this conversation was leading but wanting to hear whatever it was he felt compelled to share with her.

"It consumed my mother and I don't think she had a clue how many problems it caused me in school. Anyway, on the drive home she told me she was sorry, that she wished she'd been more of a mother and less of a Cherokee if that's what I needed from her.''

Again he returned his gaze to the coffee table. "Her words were meant to soothe, but what they did was make me feel small and I realized that I'd been punishing her with my childish rebellion for years. The path I've been walking doesn't feel right anymore.''

This time when he looked at her, his eyes were

filled with an emotion that accelerated the beat of her heart. "I'm not sure where I'm going, what new path I'll choose, but I know one thing for certain. I want you walking beside me."

He rose abruptly, grabbed her hands and pulled her to her feet. "Tamara, I can't promise you that I'll become the man in that sketch you drew. I can't promise you that I'll spend all my spare time at the cultural center. What I can promise you is that I'll keep my mind and my heart open, that I'll work on loving the part of myself that I've rejected for so long. I can promise you that I love you with every fiber of my being. Can that be enough?"

Tears half-blinded her as she reached for him. "I can't imagine not walking the path of life with you, Clay. It's enough. It's more than enough."

His lips met hers in a searing kiss. He was promising everything that he could be, promising the opening of his heart to what was important to her.

"I love you, Tamara," he said as the kiss ended.

"And I love you," she replied as a joy almost too intense to bear winged through her.

He looked around the destroyed room. "You can't stay here. I guess you'll have to come home with me."

"I guess so," she said.

"And you can forget about sleeping in the spare room. I want you beside me every night for the rest of my life." His eyes blazed with his love for her and she knew she'd found her warrior...the man who'd stolen her heart and would hold it captive forever.

Epilogue

Alyssa Whitefeather sat on a lounge chair on the James's back patio. She sipped her iced tea and reveled in the feeling of all being well.

Uncle Thomas reigned king over the barbecue grill where meat sizzled and spat. Aunt Rita was busy rearranging the rest of the food on the tables, greeting guests and doting on the men who were newcomers in their family.

Adam and Breanna sat with Maggie at a nearby table, their laughter a joyous sound riding the light breeze of the perfect August day. Breanna's tummy was beginning to show the signs of her pregnancy and Alyssa knew she'd been placed on desk duty at the police station.

Savannah and Riley had married the day before in a quiet ceremony with family only. Savannah wore the beautiful smile of a new bride as she and her husband helped Rita with the food.

Clay and Tamara stood near Thomas at the grill, Clay teasing his father about his grilling skills. Alyssa had never seen Clay look so relaxed, so happy.

It was a joyous gathering…a celebration of old love and new, of happiness. It was the celebration of a family reunited.

The serial killer was still out there, but there was no talk of those crimes today. Rita had been returned to her family and Tamara's tormentor was in jail and the conversation was pleasant and happy.

Alyssa took another sip of her tea and that's when it happened. Blindness overtook her in an instant and she heard a faint whimper escape her lips. Then she was seeing not the party, not her beloved relatives, but a man…a handsome man with black hair and ice blue eyes.

It was night and he was walking toward her, a sexy smile riding his sensual lips. Suddenly he was being stabbed…over and over again and Alyssa wasn't just a spectator to what was happening. She was a participant. She was the one stabbing him, driving the knife into his chest and she heard screaming and realized that she was making the noise, screaming in victory.

She opened her eyes, shocked to find herself still in the lounge chair, laughter ringing in the air. Her glass of iced tea was no longer in her hand but had dropped to the ground.

Thankfully, nobody had noticed that she'd been out…momentarily unconscious…lost in a horrific vision. The sound of merriment now sounded too shrill as an icy chill claimed her soul. She knew now that evil forces still surrounded Cherokee Corners and that somehow, someway, she was a part of that evil.

*   *   *   *   *

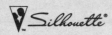

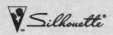

**The Wolfe twins' stories—
together in one fantastic volume!**

USA TODAY bestselling author

JOAN HOHL
Double WOLFE

The emotional story of Matilda Wolfe plus an original short
story about Matilda's twin sister, Lisa. The twins have
followed different paths...but each leads to true love!

Look for DOUBLE WOLFE in January 2004.

"A compelling storyteller who weaves her tales
with verve, passion and style."
—*New York Times* bestselling author Nora Roberts

Where love comes alive™

eHARLEQUIN.com

For **FREE online reading,** visit www.eHarlequin.com now and enjoy:

Online Reads
Read **Daily** and **Weekly** chapters from our Internet-exclusive stories by your favorite authors.

Red-Hot Reads
Turn up the heat with one of our more sensual online stories!

Interactive Novels
Cast your vote to help decide how these stories unfold...then stay tuned!

Quick Reads
For shorter romantic reads, try our collection of Poems, Toasts, & More!

Online Read Library
Miss one of our online reads? Come here to catch up!

Reading Groups
Discuss, share and rave with other community members!

For great reading online,
visit www.eHarlequin.com today!

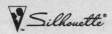

COMING NEXT MONTH

SIMCNM1203